BRING TO A BOIL
AND SEPARATE

BRING TO A BOIL AND SEPARATE

Hadley Irwin

A Margaret K. McElderry Book

ATHENEUM   1981   NEW YORK

LIBRARY OF CONGRESS CATALOGING IN PUBLICATION DATA

Irwin, Hadley.
Bring to a boil and separate.

"A Margaret K. McElderry book."
SUMMARY: Katie Wagner's world begins falling apart
during her 13th summer when her parents, both veteri-
narians, decide to divorce.
[1. Divorce—Fiction] I. Title.
PZ7.I712Br   [Fic]   79-23090
ISBN 0-689-50156-0

Published simultaneously in Canada by McClelland & Stewart, Ltd.
Manufactured by R. R. Donnelley & Sons
Crawfordsville, Indiana
Designed by Marjorie Zaum
First Printing February 1980
Second Printing February 1981

To all Carols and Jean

BRING TO A BOIL
AND SEPARATE

Chapter One

FOR FOUR WEEKS I HAD MACRAMED, LEATHER-TOOLED, beaded, hiked, dived, canoed, yes-ma'amed, smiled, sung "Itsy Bitsy Spider" and "Tell Me Why the Stars Do Shine" around the campfire, and "Day Is Done, Gone the Sun" from the tent—all without my best friend, LC.

Her name is really Marti, but she has this cherub face that makes teachers write "A Lovely Child" on her report cards, so I call her "LC."

I was camped-out and ready for home.

I should have known when I was assigned to the first session at Camp Sacajawewa and Marti to the second that my horoscope had been right: "Travel is inadvisable at this time." The only thing worse than going *to* camp without your best friend is riding back home from camp with a busload of younger kids.

I was in the back of the bus, where Marti and I usually sat. We always picked a seat next to the back window so we could make signs and hold them up to the cars behind —signs like "Honk if you believe in horns" or "Your tires are tired." Of course, we were younger then.

But when the bus stopped in Dawson and I saw Dinty waiting for me, not Mom or Dad, I wanted to turn around and go back to Camp Sacajawewa—even if the food *was* lousy and I had to share a tent with Stinky Carlin, who was twelve and still wet her bed.

I knew I was going to hate the rest of that summer more than any other time in my life.

That's not quite true. I really hated Mrs. Wherle's fifth grade more, only that was different. Everybody hated Mrs. Wherle. She'd never believe you when you put up your hand to go to the toilet; then she'd get after you for wiggling and would pinch your shoulder, digging her long red fingernails into the soft spots. And when she leaned over your desk, her breath smelled like our dog after he'd rolled in dead fish.

I was mad before I went to camp. I was ticked off at Mom and her pet clinic, at Dad and his new vet practice down at Hanway, at my brother Dinty and his pimply friends who hung out at the Drive-In and made smart cracks at the girls. And it didn't help that every other girl in my grade wore at least a size thirty-two when I could wear only a T-shirt and no one knew the difference—except me. Marti says I'm a very sensitive child, so she calls me "SC."

I was all mixed up. I'd just about given up trying to be a girl. Boys had it made. They grew up without messing around; girls had all that other stuff to go through.

I wasn't dumb and neither was Marti. We were both thirteen and read a lot.

I knew about Angie Loomis and why Mom flipped when Dinty walked her home from a basketball game. I knew enough not to sit on boys' laps (even if one asked me) or hide with them in Bourne's garage when we played Kick the Can. I knew what happened when people got married, and sometimes when they didn't.

But I wasn't sure about divorce.

Before that summer, I'd thought divorce happened only on TV or in magazines and newspapers like those columns "Can This Marriage Be Saved?" or "After Divorce." Divorce was something like dying. People did it, but never anyone you knew.

I didn't like the word then, and I don't like it now. Sometimes, if you don't put something into words, it doesn't exist. Maybe that's how Mom felt. She avoided words that summer. So did Dad. And Dinty didn't talk to anyone much until the end of the summer, and by that time I knew all about divorce.

Anyway, I climbed out of the bus. There wasn't any choice.

"Hey, Squirt. Where's your bag?" Dinty is a creep.

"Over on the curb."

"Come on. I'll carry it for you."

Somebody got mixed up on Dinty and me. Dinty has Mom's fair skin and copper hair. I have Dad's black hair and skin that looks like leather by late summer.

"Where's Mom?"

"Out on a call. Thompson's mare got tangled up in some barbed wire."

"Where's Dad?"

"Staying at Hanway."

If Dad was staying at Hanway, it *had* happened!

"Hurry up. I got other things to do."

I didn't want to go home. Where do you go when you don't want to go home?

A few months ago it was different. I couldn't wait to get home even though Mom was usually working late at the clinic. And the day Dad bought me my own horse, I skipped last hour study hall to get home. Told them I was sick.

I only lie to other people. Never to myself. There is a difference.

Oh, I cheat on my horoscope sometimes. I'm really a Libra and so is Marti, but mostly I pick the sign that has the best prediction for the day and use that. I had picked Gemini that day because it said, "Your personal projects continue to be favored." I didn't have any "personal projects" but at least it sounded better than Libra: "Avoid a situation wherein you try to please everyone and please no one."

"What you been doing, Dinty?"

He heaved my duffel bag up on his shoulder.

"Just messing around. Helping Mom in the clinic now and then. Geez, this is heavy. How many leather belts did you make this summer?"

"About nine hundred. I didn't bring any home. I was runner-up in the tennis tournament, though."

The sun was a red glow behind the houses as we turned down into Croll's Alley.

"How come you didn't win? Your moon in the wrong tent?"

Dinty thinks astrology is dumb.

"No, stupid. She used a cut serve. You know—where it just stops dead when it lands."

"Maybe you should learn how to do it. Somebody's giving tennis lessons down at the park. Starting tomorrow. Better sign up."

"Maybe I will."

Dinty kicked an empty Pepsi can from the gutter and sent it clanging down the alley.

"Why you walking so slow? Hurry up."

"I don't feel like going home."

Dinty gave the can another kick and it skittered in front of me. Before I could get my foot into position, he charged from behind and sent me sprawling sideways into Mr. Pagel's hedge.

"You dirty. . . ." It didn't do any good to use words on Dinty—nor temper, nor tears. There were times when I hated him most of all.

I pulled myself out of the bushes.

This time the Pepsi can sailed up into Mrs. Winthrop's back yard.

"I hope she saw you do that and reports you for littering and you get arrested and have to pay a hundred dollar fine," I shouted at him.

"So?"

"So what?"

"So why are you such a pain? What's eating you? You going through some adolescent phase?"

"No. I'm not going through a phase. And it's none of your business, anyway. You didn't have to come after me. I could have carried my own stuff home."

"Great. Then carry it." He tossed my duffel bag at me. "Why didn't you stay in camp?"

"I was thinking about it."

"Thinking? You thinking? Now I've heard everything."

"Yes, I was thinking. Even thinking about running away."

I hadn't been thinking of running away, but sometimes threats like that work on Dinty.

"Oh. That's sharp. Real sharp." He leaned against Mrs. Winthrop's fence, fished a cigarette out of his shirt pocket, and rolled it between his thumb and forefinger. Mom would have grounded him for a week if she knew he carried cigarettes. I filed the information for future use.

"No kidding? Were you really thinking of cutting out?" He lit the cigarette. "I tried that once when I was little. Packed all my clothes. Got as far as Wright's corner and my wagon tipped over. Changed my mind. Never tried it again."

"Scared?"

"No. The farther I went, the worse I felt. And where was there to go? I went home."

"That's what I'm trying to tell you, stupid. It's . . . awful . . . when you don't want to go home and there's nowhere else to go."

"How come you don't want to go home?"

"I dunno. Marti's at camp for the next four weeks. And nobody's around. Mom and Dad are usually on their way to someplace else."

"They can't help it. That vet quitting over at Hanway doubled Dad's work, and Mom doesn't dare leave the pet clinic."

"I know. But you'd think. . . ."

"You think too much. Try winging it."

"You need wings."

"Grow some." He knocked the ash off with a flick of one finger.

"It's Mom and Dad."

"What about Mom and Dad?"

"If they'd just come out and fight like they used to."

"That was before you left for camp. You should hear them now. Down at the clinic when they think they're alone."

"They fight?"

"They yell. It sure sounds like a fight."

I knew things weren't right with Mom and Dad before I left, more because of what they didn't do than what they did. I asked Mom about it one night.

"How come Dad's never home?"

"He's busy."

"Every night?"

"Most every night. Don't worry about it, Kate."

But it did worry me, because I was part of *them*.

Dinty finally put out his cigarette with the toe of his sneaker and picked up my bag, and we walked along together, not talking.

Sometimes, when I'm alone and the streets are quiet, I pretend that I'm the only person left alive. You can blow your mind thinking that. I look around and whatever I see belongs to me. After all, I'm the only person left in the world. I can do anything I want . . . borrow Dinty's sleeping bag without asking, ride my horse across anybody's yard, stay up all night, hop in a car and drive to the Drive-In and have all the flavors of ice cream at once.

But then I always get to the point where if I had everything, I really wouldn't want anything anymore. I never could figure that out, because in real life I want everything and I want everything to be right. That's because I'm a Libra. My horoscope book says that the sign of Libra is the scales and they stand for love of peace, justice, and harmony. Instead I was coming home to what Marti would call "gorilla warfare."

"We've already eaten." Dinty threw my duffel bag down on the back step.

"Mom too?"

"Yep. She left some stuff out on the table. I'll feed Denver, if you want."

Denver is my horse.

"Don't bother." I paused by the back door. "I'm not hungry."

"Okay. Have it your way. Tell Mom I'll be down at the Drive-In with some of the guys."

I walked across the back yard, climbed the fence, and crossed the pasture lot to the barn.

Denver snorted when he saw me.

"I'll bet you're hungry, old fellow."

Grain clung to his underlip and his water pail was full. Mom must have fed and watered him. The palomino pushed his head against my shoulder. I hugged him, wishing he had arms to hug me back. He remembered me after four weeks, and that's pretty good for a horse.

I climbed up and sat on the top rail of the fence while Denver finished. He'd eaten his oats and was starting in on the hay. Denver's like me. He likes his dessert first. That way you get the best first and sometimes you don't have to eat the hay.

I began talking to him. That's another nice thing about horses. They listen. You can tell the way they flick their ears. And they never interrupt or make smart remarks —like Dinty.

So I told Denver why I'd been away so long and all about summer camp and how much fun parts of it were and how awful the food had been and all about the tennis tournament and how I almost won.

Then I told him what I couldn't say to Dinty.

"They're going to do it, Denver. They *are* going to get a divorce. I know they are. That's why Dad's staying in Hanway instead of driving down every day like he did before I left. And, Denver, I feel awful. Down in the bottom of my stomach. And I'm not hungry. How would you like it, Denver, if you'd been away and came home and the whole barn was gone and there was nobody here to take care of you? You'd feel divorced, too. That's how I feel. Divorced. It's like they're divorcing *me*. Me and Dinty. Not each other. Do you know what'll happen, Denver? I'll grow up having psychological problems. I'll be emotionally scarred. I just know it."

I stopped talking and began to wonder how you could tell if someone had emotional scars. Probably not until after the person died. Then if you'd cut open their heads there'd be lots of little white lines on their brains.

I put my hand on my forehead to see if I could feel anything happening. Then I made a fist, stuck it under my chin, and looked up at the sky. I saw Katherine Hepburn do that once in a movie called *Little Women*. She's my favorite actress, and not just because we have the same name.

Marti says I'm a weirdo when it comes to old movies. I watch them late at night in my room. I sneak the portable out of the den and watch way past midnight, with my lights out. When I was a little kid I made it a rule that I could watch old movies only in black and white. It's a good rule, really. If you watch them in color, you sometimes forget they're not real. That can be very confusing for a child.

I have another rule about old movies too. If the movie looks like it won't end happily, I turn off the TV and make up my own ending. Like *The Bride of Frankenstein* . . . when Elsa Lanchester—she's the monster's wife—sees him for the first time, she screams. I quit right there because there was no way things could work out right.

Denver knew all this because he is the one I tell my picture endings to.

I could see that Denver was bored since I'd stopped talking. It was getting late and I hadn't unpacked my stuff from camp, and besides I couldn't feel any scars yet, so I told him good night and slid off the fence.

I went back into the house and emptied my duffel bag in the middle of the kitchen floor. The clothes smelled dirty and mildewed, so I stuck them in the washer. In the middle of the pile, wrapped up in my Camp Sacajawewa T-shirt, were the presents I'd brought for Mom and Dad. I used to bring them the same things every year—belts in different colors. They both had four beaded belts hanging in their big closet. This year I made them something different—beaded rings.

After I started the washer, I took my runner-up tennis badge and the matching beaded rings and stuffed them in the bottom of my dresser drawer under my winter sweaters. I banged the drawer shut and decided I wouldn't give either one of them their present this year.

The house was quiet and empty. I went back to the kitchen. The stuff Mom had left out was wilted and shrunk.

I got a glass of milk. Dinty had left the carton out again.
I still wasn't hungry.

I poured the lukewarm milk down the drain and stared
out the window, past Mom's ivy that hung like a limp
question mark from the macrame halter I'd made in camp
the summer before.

Marti would have said, "Sensitive Child, you're suffering from a Deep Purple Funk."

Chapter Two

WHEN YOU'RE ALONE IN AN EMPTY HOUSE AND YOU don't want to think, there are only two things you can do: watch TV or read. The voices on TV sound human, so I usually turn on the set in the den and sit in the living room and read. That way I have two things going on at once—the voices on TV that don't say anything much and the voices in the book that talk louder than real people and make more sense.

There are other voices, though—my inside voices. They're often the loudest. Sometimes they drown out both the TV and the book. I tried to tell Dinty about it once, but he said I'd better watch out or they'd cart me off to a looney farm.

That night, waiting for Mom to come home, I was reading one of her psychology magazines and it said, "The supreme communication of life is sex."

Marti would have loved that.

My voices really started talking then.

"They don't teach *that* in eighth grade Communication Skills. Not even in basics."

"Marti says they lie to you in school."

"And leave out all the really interesting things."

"They're afraid you'll learn too much too fast. You're supposed to learn just what they tell you."

"Afraid you'll read a chapter ahead and upset the curriculum."

My voices were getting real loud when I heard Mom's car in the drive. My clothes were still in the dryer. I had forgotten them.

I was pulling out a pair of wrinkled shorts when Mother walked in. Only it was not Mother. It was Dr. Helen Warner, who happens to be my mother. It always takes her a little while to switch when she gets home.

When I was little, I thought she had two faces, one for home and one for work. I thought she kept her extra face on one of those spooky white Styrofoam heads you use for wigs. Even her hands were different—one set for combing snarls out of my hair and another set for scalpels and surgical needles. I used to believe she hung her hands in the back of the closet and changed them when I wasn't around.

"Hi," I said as Mom came in. "I'm home."

For a minute she stood and looked at me so hard I wondered if I'd changed into someone else while I was at camp. Then she hugged me tight. That doesn't happen often in our family—the hugging. It's not that we don't love each other; it's more as if no one ever thinks of taking time to do it. That night the hug felt good.

"Did you just get here? How was camp?"

Mom plugged in the coffeepot. She goes for a cup of coffee like an accident victim for a blood transfusion. It would save her time if she'd fill one of those bottle and tube things they use in hospitals and strap it to her arm.

I repeated the same stuff about camp I'd told Denver. Usually when Mom gets home, she collapses in a chair, but tonight it was as if she couldn't sit still. She wiped off the counter, even though I'd already done that, put the dishes away, and watered her plants. Then she noticed the clothes I'd washed.

"Oh, Katie, you *didn't* leave those things in the dryer? They'll have to be washed through again to get the wrinkles out."

Dr. Warner had disappeared, and Mother was home for sure.

For once, I didn't sigh and roll my eyes and say, "Oh, Moth—ther!" I just nodded. It felt good that some things were the same as before I'd left for camp.

Marti says a child needs that. She says it's called "blanket security." Marti gets ninety-nine percent on the vocabulary part of the Basic Skills Tests.

Mom finally sat down and looked at her coffee cup, but I don't think she was seeing it.

"Your father's in Hanway."

I remember thinking, "Okay. Here it comes." I gritted my teeth and barely opened my mouth. "Yea, I know. Dinty told me. When'll he be back?"

"Tomorrow morning. To see you. But there's something I have to tell you. About your father and me."

Now she was looking everywhere except at me.

Did she really think I didn't know? Did she think it was a surprise? I'd been at camp for four weeks and she'd written four letters and never mentioned Dad. And Dad had called me once, which he'd never done before, and he hadn't said anything about Mom. How dumb did they think I was?

So I just nodded.

Marti says you can confuse any issue by nodding.

"Katie. We've separated."

I wanted to giggle. Crazy, I know, at one of the most important moments of my life, but I wanted to giggle. All I could see were the instructions on a spaghetti box—"Bring to boil and separate."

Then the next second I felt like crying.

"What's going to happen?" It didn't sound like my voice.

She looked at me as if I'd asked when the world was going to end. Maybe that's what I *was* asking.

"Honey, we don't know. We're trying very hard to find out."

"Why didn't you tell me before. Before I left for camp? Why did you wait until I was gone?"

They'd always made this big deal about the truth and this sure didn't fit.

She poured another cup of coffee, and I knew she was trying to think of something to say. I'd done that with her lots of times.

"We didn't know it was going to happen this fast. We weren't trying to lie to you."

How could she know exactly what I was thinking?

"But what will happen to *me*? Dinty and me?"

"Nothing. We'll live here. Your father will stay in Hanway. There's an apartment behind his office." It was her Dr. Warner voice.

"Doesn't he love us any more?"

"That has nothing to do with it."

"Don't *you* love him anymore?"

She rubbed her forehead, elbows resting on the table. "In a way." Her voice sounded old and tired, like Ethel Barrymore's.

"How can you love someone all your life and then *not* love someone?" My voice kept going higher and I couldn't stop it. "How can you quit loving a family? We're a family."

Mom went on in a tired, dead voice as if she hadn't even heard me. "When we were young, everyone expected us to get married. We thought we believed in the same things. When we were together, lights flashed and bells rang—I can't explain, Katie. The lights went out. Does that make any sense?"

Of course it didn't. It sounded like an amusement park with the electricity off.

"Don't *you* want us either? Dinty and me?"

"Don't be silly. Of course, I want you. And so does your father. I told you. You have nothing to do with it. Nothing at all."

"Oh, sure." It was almost a sob, but I wrapped my arms around my stomach and held the sound inside.

"It would have been worse without you and Dinty. Katie, good things take time to grow. Bad things happen fast. Or at least recognizing that things are bad can happen fast. That's how it was with your father and me. Can you understand at all?"

"Sort of." And I could. Losing the tennis tournament

at camp had happened all at once. I thought I had it won. Then pow, pow. Two bad backhands in a row, and I lost.

I learned long ago that if you don't want to talk about a certain thing, it's smart to talk about *anything* else. So I finished folding my camp clothes, slammed the dryer shut, and asked, "How's the mare?"

"The mare? Oh, Thompson's mare. She'll be all right." She gulped her coffee. "Where's Dinty?"

"Where he always is. Down at the Drive-In."

"He should be home." She brushed her hand through her hair.

I used to love the feel of her hair. It was thick and cushy and I could lose my fingers in it.

I couldn't help thinking about the times when Dad and Mom and I would be sitting at the kitchen table and Mom would say the very same thing. "Where's Dinty?" but to Dad, not me. I got the same feeling in my stomach that I'd had when I saw Dinty waiting for me at the bus station. I turned and walked over to the sink.

"Katie? Do you feel all right?"

"I'm okay," I muttered.

"Maybe you'd better run on up to bed. It's been a long day."

"I'm not tired."

She didn't want me around, I knew. And it would be long after midnight before she would go to bed.

"What will you do tomorrow?" Her spoon made half circles in her coffee.

"Dinty told me they're giving tennis lessons in the park. The paper says it costs two dollars an hour for six lessons." I didn't turn around.

"I'll leave a check on the desk. Katie . . . it's good to

see your back." It was an old family joke, but neither of us laughed.

I heard her rinsing her coffee cup under the faucet as I unplugged the TV in the den and took it up to my room. I shut my bedroom door and locked it.

One thing I knew for sure. I was never going to grow up to be a mother.

I lay face down on my bed and wondered what happened to girls to turn them into mothers—besides having children. Mom had some pictures in her photo album of when she was about my age. There was this whole bunch of kids trying to see how many could pile into a VW, and Mom was laughing and her hair was messed up and she had her arms around two other girls, one on each side of her, and their arms were around her and she looked as if she'd be fun to know. What changed her? She hardly ever laughed now, and if she did, her laugh came out in pieces.

Then I started thinking that if there was a Dr. Warner and if there was a mother, then maybe there was someone else too—someone I didn't know or even Dad didn't know —hidden in that photograph.

It was funny. The past year Dad had started calling her "Mom" too or "your mother," as if she belonged to me. When I was smaller, it had been "Elly" or "Lena" or sometimes "Agnes." I could never figure out "Agnes," but it always made Mom blush and laugh. Those names, and the other people Mom must have been, had disappeared.

Can you erase people by taking away their names?

Chapter Three

I WOKE EARLY THE NEXT MORNING, BUT MOM AND DINTY had already left the house. I hadn't stayed up late because the only movie on TV was one with Bette Davis called *Dark Victory*. When the story begins she has a brain tumor and that didn't sound as if it could have a happy ending. I like Bette Davis a whole lot, but I've never seen the end of any of her pictures. I guess she never made any happy ones.

Anyway, I was eating breakfast food and checking out the horoscopes in the morning paper. It was a tough choice between being a Scorpio—"good day for new activities" and a Leo—"expect the unexpected."

"Hey, Skeeter!" It was Dad and I hadn't even heard his pickup. He burst through the door and stood grinning at me.

Now Mom can slip into a room and no one notices, but when she leaves, you miss her right away.

Dad looked older, and the grin he was giving me didn't quite reach his eyes, but I smiled back. "There's still some coffee left. Would you like some?"

"Sure."

He ruffled my hair as he passed. "Well, Skeeter. I hear you were almost a tennis champion."

Only Dad calls me Skeeter. He says I remind him of a mosquito, always buzzing but never going anywhere. Dinty says it's because I carry disease.

I went through the camp routine again as I had with Mom the night before. I didn't have to think much about what I was saying and it was a safe topic. Both of them always thought they were doing me this big favor with the summer camp bit. They'd say stuff like "a sound mind in a sound body" or "good health is the way to happiness." Marti calls it brain-washing.

I replayed the tennis game for the third time and watched Dad. Just like Mom, he sat and stared at his coffee cup as if it were something under a microscope. Not only would I have scars on my brain, but if I took after him, I'd be bug-eyed. I wondered if there were eye exercises to prevent it.

When the tennis finally ran out, we just sat there for a couple of minutes until the stillness got uncomfortable. Then we both started talking at the same time.

"I'm going to start tennis . . ."

"Don't forget about the barrel races . . ."

Dad has a bigger voice, so he won and went right on talking. "If you're going to enter Denver, you're going to have to practice. Not just once in a while, but every day."

"I know." I thought about saluting, but he wasn't in the mood to think it funny, and I didn't want him to laugh just because he thought he had to.

Barrel races. I had agreed to enter to please Mom and Dad. I'd won pole-bending the year before, and it was taken for granted that I'd do the barrels this summer. Besides it had given them something to talk about when there wasn't anything else to say.

"I'll start this afternoon. I promise. What time will you be home?"

The last part slipped out by itself. I felt my face getting red and something pushing up inside the back of my throat.

"Skeeter." Once again he was doing what Mom did—looking past me. If this kept up, I'd be cross-eyed. "I'll be down in Hanway. There's a lot to take care of there."

He didn't so much stop. It was more as if his voice faded out. If I'd done that, he'd have accused me of side-stepping the issue, but as Marti says, "Parent-made rules do not apply to parents." Besides, it was an issue I *wanted* to sidestep.

"Yea, sure. I mean I know you're busy and all." I made a big deal of tipping up my bowl and drinking the last of the milk.

Dad said automatically, "What's wrong with your spoon?" That's what he always said, and we were safely off the subject. And then he added, "Skeeter. You and I should have a little talk one of these days."

There's nothing worse than a parent having a *little* talk, even if you don't know what they want to talk about. It's never ever about anything good.

"Great. But not now. I've got to sign up for tennis lessons."

"I didn't mean this very minute. Anyway, I have to get to work."

"Oh."

I practically never say "oh." It's an adult word. Marti calls it a *"non sec quiter."*

At least the "oh" worked, because the conversation quit and I was glad.

Dad punched me in the arm and left, and I went down to the barn to feed and groom Denver. I like to groom Denver. The morning sun can turn his coat into the most beautiful golden cream. I gave him a lump of sugar and he nosed my pocket for more.

"One lump's enough. Do you want to lose your teeth?" But I didn't want to talk to anyone—not even Denver. He watched, giving me time to change my mind, then turned and trotted toward the barn.

I didn't feel like grooming him. I didn't feel like doing anything. It was as if I'd been to the dentist, and he'd frozen my tooth only the freezing covered my whole body. I felt cut off, and although the barn was there and the new fence and the pasture and Denver, they were no longer real.

Of course, the house was empty when I got back, but it felt even emptier than the night before and I had an hour to kill before sign-up time for tennis lessons.

That's a terrible thing—to kill an hour. It's like throwing away little pieces of your life. Marti says it's a "sin of omission." I wanted to live the hour, but that's not easy in an empty house.

I thought of doing something to please Mom, like cleaning the kitchen floor, but I had on clean white shorts.

Why do they always picture angels in white? You can't do good deeds dressed that way.

I went into the den to get the check Mom had left. It was there, but she had either forgotten what I told her or she hadn't been listening because she hadn't filled in the amount. It was made out to the "City Recreation Program." I started to write in "twelve" but I stopped with "t-w-e." I could write it for twenty. All it took was three different letters at the end—n-t-y instead of l-v-e.

I did it as quickly as the thought passed through my mind.

I had no idea what I wanted the extra money for. Anyway, it wasn't the money that was important. It was the way I felt, as if I had opened my mouth, thrown back my head, and yelled. I could almost hear the sound echo through the house. And I felt good. Really good, for the first time since I'd come home from camp.

I dashed out of the house. It was a bright morning. The birds were making summery sounds, and the row of maples turned Forest Street into a shadowy tunnel.

I ran all the way to the park.

When I got there, kids were already lined up in front of two tables beside the tennis courts. On one side were the little kids, not much bigger than their rackets, and on the other side kids about my age. Some of them I recognized from school—the ones you just say "hi" to and that's where it ends. Marti, of course, was up doing her time at Camp Sacajawewa. I joined the line, clutching my check.

Laura Dobbs was taking the money. She knew Mom, so I handed her my check—and pocketed the extra eight dollars she gave me.

"Arrange a time with Joan over there." She pointed at

a tanned girl sitting cross-legged on the grass cradling a clip board.

"Get yourself new tennis balls, Kathryn," the girl ordered in a voice that matched her sun-blonde hair. She had a white sweatband across her forehead, and I began to get excited about tennis. Half of getting excited about anything is all the stuff you can buy—like new tennis balls, sweatbands, and rackets. I had eight dollars. I could spend the rest of the morning shopping for equipment, and the extra eight dollars could easily be explained to Mom. "When they told me all the stuff I had to have, I made the check out for twenty," I rehearsed what I'd say when Mom went through her month's checks. I never used to do that—rehearse what I was going to say to Mom—until that summer.

So I bought a can of tennis balls and a magazine on tennis and was waiting at the cash register for a clerk, but he was busy. There on the counter were sweatbands—just like Joan's. There were wristbands, too, made of the same material.

I slipped one on my right wrist, just to see how it felt. A wristband wouldn't be copying.

The clerk came up to the counter. I laid down the can of balls and the magazine and handed him six dollars.

"Signing up for lessons?"

I nodded.

He placed the can and the magazine in a sack and stapled on the sales slip. I didn't mention the wristband.

I felt a secret tingle run from my stomach down through the back of my legs. I could hardly keep from grinning. I wasn't stealing. I was just ripping it off. I felt as if I had won something. I didn't know what I had won or who I had won over, but it was the feeling that counted.

And I liked the feeling.

That's about when the summer came apart. Those first couple of days after I got home from camp were connected, the way days are supposed to be. What happened one day led into what happened the next, and I could keep track of where I was and who I was and what was going on. But then things came unglued. I felt like two Kates—one marked "His" and one marked "Hers."

Chapter Four

MOM AND DAD AND DINTY AND I DRIFTED ALONG FOR A while without talking about what was happening to us. Dad stayed at Hanway, and I tried to pretend he was just off to a convention or some short course and that he'd be back in a week or so.

There used to be this program on TV called *Father Knows Best*. Whenever *they* had a problem, they'd all sit around the dining room table and talk. It was a dumb program. Marti says that's what is dangerous about TV. They romanticize. I'm not sure what that means exactly, but I like the sound of the word.

Marti's exceptional. She really is. Even Mrs. Wherle says she's a gifted child. Marti can sit in math class and read a library book and when Mr. Norton asks her a question, she can answer and go right back to her book and never lose her place. She says she does it to "counteract the establishment."

Anyway our family *didn't* sit around the dining room table and our family *didn't* talk about our problem. At least they didn't until Grandfather arrived, but that was later.

I'd also discovered that if you looked busy with healthy, outdoor things, parents would ignore you and figure you were being a normal kid and they didn't have to worry. That was fine with me. I didn't want to be worried about, and I didn't want any little talks with Dad or any more with Mom. So I watched the late late movies, slept all morning, played tennis in the afternoons, and worked Denver through the barrels in the evening, but the days were hollow.

One day, I was down by the barn, sitting under the willow watching Denver munch grass—and thinking. It was a different world under the willow. When the breeze swept through the drooping branches, Denver and the grass and the barn and the sky turned into a mixture of cream and green and red, spattered on blue.

Dad had only been home a couple of times to pick up some clothes, and Mom had been busier than usual at the clinic. I think they tried not to be in the house at the same time. Not that it made much difference. Before I left for camp, they could be in the same room together and act as if each of them were alone.

Of course, Dinty was never around. He helped Mom at the clinic during the day and hung around the Drive-In at night. For a while I thought he was smoking pot or something. He acted spacier than usual. So I looked through all his drawers and his closet, but the only things I found were a couple of stale cigarettes and a sexy magazine. If I were going to have emotional scars, the least he could do was to get mixed up with drugs. I decided he wasn't as sensitive as I.

Just then Dinty yelled at me and vaulted the board fence. He was on the track team at school and liked to show off.

"Hey, champ! I've been looking all over for you. Are you a champeen jock or a champeen jockey today?"

It was not easy to like Dinty.

He flopped down beside me and fired a handful of dirt and grass that hit me just above my right ear and dribbled down inside my shirt.

"Okay, grouch. I was teasing."

I brushed the grass out of my hair. Silence could drive Dinty crazy.

"You work Denver out today?"

"Not yet. Too hot."

"Excuses, excuses. Never win the barrels that way."

"So?"

"So. How are the tennis lessons?"

"The first day was a bummer. Got in with a bunch of little kids. Spent the whole morning learning how to hold a racket. And Kendall—she's the instructor, always hollering: 'No. Do it this way. You're off-balance. Your grip is wrong.' I learned all that years ago."

"Why not quit?"

"I almost did. I was the only one who could get the ball back across the net. And she still kept yelling. Like Mom."

"Nobody yells like Mom." Dinty rolled over on his back and closed his eyes.

"But I'm going to get private lessons two days a week from now on. She's a Libra, too."

"Who?"

"Joan, stupid."

"Who's Joan Stupid?"

"Joan Kendall, the instructor."

Dinty yawned. "What's that got to do with tennis?"

"I dunno. But it's interesting."

"What about the barrels? You need a lot of work. And some help from Mom. She's good."

"I know. I know. I'll ask her. Give me time. Say, what time is it?"

"Around five-thirty. Why?"

"Whose turn to get dinner?"

"Yours, lucky. That's what I came to tell you. I'm going to Hanway to help Dad for a while. The office is a mess—needs cleaning and painting and stuff."

"How come you get to go and not me? I can do just as much as you can."

"You've got your tennis and Denver to worry about. Besides I need the money. Dad's paying me. Gotta start saving for college."

"Well, I'm going to college too."

Dinty stood up and punched me in the shoulder like a boxer. "I'm older. That makes college closer. See? If it were the other way around, then you'd need the job first."

I hated Dinty most when he was being reasonable.

I pinched off a blade of grass, down at the root where the green faded into pale white and swallowed twice to make my voice come out right.

"Dinty, are they going to get a divorce?" I sounded a

little bit like Elizabeth Taylor in *National Velvet*. That was in color, but I'd watched it anyway.

He squinted at me for a minute and then looked away. "Your guess is as good as mine. Look. I don't want to talk about it."

"I know. But they can't do it without telling us, can they? I mean, we have rights too, don't we? We're citizens."

"Okay. Okay. I think they're going to go through with it. I don't think they've made up their minds yet, and that's why they haven't said anything to us. There's nothing we can do about it, anyhow."

"But we'll be orphans."

"Oh, for Pete's sake. You watch too many movies."

"At least, if they *do* get a divorce, we won't have to hear them fight anymore."

"I gotta go."

"Is Dad picking you up?"

"I'm catching the bus. I'll be back this weekend."

He climbed the fence and walked slowly toward the house. I waited until I heard the front door slam, then I followed.

What would I fix for supper? Mom didn't care as long as it was well-balanced. My menus usually came out that way—well-balanced—lettuce on one end, vegetable at the other, and a hamburger in the middle.

By seven, dinner was finished and Mom was sipping her third cup of coffee.

"Well, shall we take Denver out and see what he can do?"

I was getting so I could read Mom's moods as easily as she could read a thermometer. She'd had a good day.

Maybe she was glad Dinty was gone for the week. Maybe she was glad Dad was gone too.

"Don't you have to go back to the office?"

"Not tonight." Mom looked younger, more relaxed than usual. Her hair shone where the sun from the window struck it and her eyes were soft. I thought of the girl in the photograph.

"Okay. I'll go down and tack up."

I said that I lie only to other people. I'd kind of lied to Dinty, because I had been working Denver sometimes in the afternoon and even in the mornings. We must have made that figure eight a hundred times, first slow and then fast.

Barrel racing isn't as easy as it looks, even on a horse like Denver. He'd gone fine at first, but then he'd started rushing the barrels, going too fast and making the turns too quickly. Maybe I'd leaned too far on the inside of the turns. Anyway he slipped with me once and we went down. I didn't tell anyone about it, but afterward, things weren't the same. Denver still ran, but I could tell he didn't like it.

The session with Mom went the way I knew it would. She sat on the top rail, her coffee cup in hand and watched. I took Denver around the ring, backed him, put him through figure eights and the flying changes that he hated. Then we ran the barrels.

"He's soured, Kate. What happened?"

I'll never understand how sometimes mothers don't know anything and the next minute they know everything.

I rode Denver over to the fence and slipped out of the saddle.

"Did you two go down?"

I ran my fingers through Denver's mane.

"I said, did you fall?"

"Yeah. A few days ago. But we didn't get hurt."

"Thought so." Mom got off the fence and deposited her coffee cup by a post. She took the reins from me and stroked Denver's sleek neck, cradling his nose in the crook of her arm. I always thought she could talk to animals. Anyway, they always did what she wanted.

"You can't always *fix* things, Katie." She loosed the girth and pulled off the saddle. "But you can start over."

"Start over! There isn't time."

"There's always time to try." She finished untacking and slapped Denver on the rump. "You don't have to cool him down. He hasn't worked that hard."

"But how do I begin all over? All that wasted time."

"Nothing is ever wasted, Katie . . . in this life. But there's no percentage in trying to patch up a bad performance. What you will have to do is start over, go back to the beginning. Reteach him the pattern again. It's too late tonight, but tomorrow we can start."

I felt I was taking a unit test in history and I hadn't read the chapter.

"What do I do?"

"You start out walking. And thinking about how Denver feels when he's running the barrels. You walk him through the pattern. Over and over again until that figure eight is fixed in his head."

I traced the figure eight in my mind. What's more boring than a figure eight done over and over again?

We were walking toward the house. The first evening star had just appeared in the western sky.

"It'll take time and patience. But Denver knew it once. He can learn again."

Mom sighed and sat down on the back porch steps.

"You see, what you're trying to do with Denver is make him forget how he broke the pattern—when he slipped. He remembers every time he comes up to that one barrel. That's why he breaks his pace. Now if you can take him back and let him walk through every barrel, he'll gain confidence and when you start to run him again, he'll have forgotten about the slip. At least that's the way it is with horses."

"But what if he slips again?"

"It's an odd thing about patterns. It's easy to break a good pattern, but hard to break a bad one."

I listened, but I knew there was no way I was going to take Denver clear back and start him over again. It would be as boring as copying over a five-page English theme, and that's B-O-R-I-N-G.

"Okay. I'll start tomorrow."

"Good girl. Your father's coming up for the races."

"Swell."

I walked around the house and went in the front door, feeling like a bad performance myself. Marti would have gagged.

Chapter Five

THE HORSE SHOW CAME FASTER THAN I WANTED IT TO. Our Saline County Horse Show goes on every year down at the old fairgrounds, and the gymkhana is always scheduled last.

It would be well after ten before Denver and I hit the barrels, and I worried how he'd react to the bright lights and the crowd noises.

Dad came up for the show. He got home just in time to fire up the grill.

"You're late," Mom said when he came into the kitchen and dropped the steaks on the table. "We've got to get that horse down there at least two or three hours before the event. He's got to be settled down and calm."

"Couldn't be helped," Dad answered. That's the way he usually answered Mom. "We'll make it in time."

I liked the sound of the "we."

He went out to the grill. I followed him and perched on the end of the picnic table and watched. Everyone in town called him Doc. He looked like a Doc. On the other hand, he could pass as a coach for the Green Bay Packers. Everything about him was big: feet, hands, neck, laugh, only he hadn't laughed for a long time. Not at home, anyway.

It was only the second time that summer we'd cooked out. Other summers we'd done it almost every night, with neighbors dropping in and bringing their steaks for Dad to grill.

Marti called him "Bigfoot," but that was when we were PDPing—Putting Down Parents. There was something about Dad, though. When things got fouled up, he could straighten them out. Like the time he took me to my first boy-girl party when I was in seventh grade. I stepped out of the car and slammed the door on the hem of my dress and ripped it. Dad put me back in the car, drove down to his office and sewed it up with suture thread.

The steaks were beginning to sizzle on the grill. Dad looked up and winked at me but didn't say anything. My parents were always so different. If anything bad happened, he'd say "That's life," and grin and shrug his shoulders. Mom had to go into the how's and why's. I guess you could say Mom is a circle. Dad is a straight line. And me? That summer I didn't know which I was, and I didn't know how to choose between them.

Dinner was awful. Even though we were all doing the things we usually did, except that Dinty was still in the shower, the whole thing was phony as a rubber duck. We were all going through motions, pretending to be a family. The steak was tough because Dad tried to hurry to please

Mom. But the conversation was worse, full of awkward spots when nobody talked and clumps when everybody said something at the same time.

"I'll go down and get Denver ready," I finally said.

"She's worried," I heard Mom say.

"She'll be all right," Dad grunted. "If she doesn't push him too hard."

The collar of my western shirt was a band of hot steel and my white cowboy hat felt as if it would fall off if I moved my head. Denver and I waited our turn at the barrels. I wished Marti were around to make me laugh. Marti could always make me laugh. She didn't have to say anything. I could just look at her and laugh.

Dad had given Denver a swat on the rump and wished us luck before he went up into the grandstand. Mom stayed with me, holding the bridle and scratching Denver's cheekbone.

"Watch the clock, Katie. It's the clock you're trying to beat."

I nodded and looked up into the grandstand to see if I could find Dad.

I did. He was sitting with—Joan Kendall.

They were in the top row and they were laughing and talking and not even looking at the arena.

I felt as if someone had hit me in the stomach. I didn't want Mom to see them. He looked happy, the way he used to. How did he know Joan? She'd never told me she knew my dad. I wondered where else they'd been together. But I didn't have time to think any more about them.

The loudspeaker was blaring, "Entry six. Kathryn Warner riding Denver."

Mom let go of the bridle and the gate opened.

"Don't push him." I heard Dad's warning again as I kicked Denver in the flanks and we burst into the circle of light and dust.

The first turn was a beaut, with Denver taking his lead as if I had taken him back to the beginning and had been walking figure eights for months. Marti would have called it a real "Can Cruncher."

The second barrel was smooth but not close enough to save the precious second that I needed to pick up. We headed back for the last turn.

"Move him, Katie. Move!" It was Mom.

Automatically I pressed my heels into Denver's flanks. This was where he had slipped before.

"Go!" I heard Dinty roar.

For a split second Denver broke his pace. His nose almost touched the barrel, but I yanked him around and gave him another good dig in the flanks, and we cleared the last barrel by inches.

I readjusted my weight and we shot out of the arena. The last burst of speed should have gained us a second, but I knew by heeling him on the last turn I had risked everything. I heard the applause from the grandstand, but I knew we were not in the money. You can't break a pattern and expect to win. I was third.

Dinty held Denver as I slipped from the saddle. "Not bad, kid. At least you didn't goof."

From Dinty that was a compliment.

"Next year," Mom said as we cooled Denver down. "It's that second run that he's afraid of. But we can take care of that next summer. I thought we could cure everything by starting over."

"Horses are dumb," I muttered, trying to swallow the

losing along with the picture of Dad sitting beside Joan Kendall.

"I guess people are dumb too," Mom looked down at me. "To think bad performances can be patched up by starting over." I thought she was talking about Denver. I wasn't sure.

I threw my cowboy hat in the front seat of the pickup and turned to see where Dad was. He finally came, threading his way through the crowd. Alone. He wasn't hard to see; he towered over everyone else. A man in a yellow seed corn cap grabbed his arm, shouted something in his ear, and slapped him on the back. Dad laughed, shook his head, and came up to me, his face flushing beneath his tan.

"Not bad, Skeeter. Not bad. You didn't win, but you made a good try." He put his arm around my shoulder and guided me over to the truck.

"Skeeter and I are going to walk home." He could have been announcing it over the loudspeaker. He rested one hand on the door. "Dinty, can you and your mother manage Denver?"

If it were a chance to drive the pickup, Dinty would agree to anything.

Mom nodded, and Dad and I watched as they drove out of the parking lot.

We walked down the river road. "The perfect short-cut for a tired old man and a third-place barrel-dodger."

I didn't comment. I didn't want to admit either was true.

The sounds from the fairgrounds faded. Dad's boots beat out a heavy rhythm as I tried to match his steps. I knew he was waiting for me to say something, but my mind was shriveled and dry.

"The voice of the locust is heard in the land," Dad boomed.

"It's the voice of the *turtle*, Dad." I knew that from a movie—*The Moon Is Blue.*

"Tonight it's locusts. Listen. When I was a kid walking home alone, I'd hear them. Them and a stray cricket or two and maybe some peepers. It sure can make for one big lonely sound, can't it?"

Again I did not answer. What could he know about loneliness? He was making my lone-ness.

"How do you know her?" I blurted.

He broke his step.

"Who's her?"

"Joan Kendall. You were sitting with her."

"Oh. The tennis pro. Is that her name?" He grinned.

"Yeah. That's her name." I was not grinning.

"She's quite a girl."

"A college girl. Where'd you meet her?"

He stopped. I walked on.

"Where'd you meet her?" he mimicked me. "I met her when I sat down next to her. She knew I was your father, and she was telling me how good a tennis player you're getting to be."

I stopped then and waited for him to catch up to me. I felt ashamed, but the next instant I knew I didn't care about barrel races or tennis lessons or anything else in the world except Dad.

I turned toward him. "Could I come and live with you?"

The road ended at a fence. Dad spread the barbed wire and I crawled through.

"I want to live with you. I need you." I waited for him to crawl through. "I love you."

The words, pinched and shrill, sounded as if they had come from a soap opera. I so wanted them to sound breathless and husky like a Hepburn.

I felt his hand, then, heavy on my shoulder.

"Which one do you mean?"

"Which one what?"

"Which one? I *need* you? Or I *love* you?"

"What's the difference?"

"A big difference, Kathryn."

"I can't see any."

"There's no *need* in loving. I love you because you're *you*. Not because I *need* you. I don't *need* you. Can you understand?"

"No." It was not a Hepburn voice. It wasn't even a soap opera voice. It was a little girl voice. He didn't *need* me. He didn't *want* me. He didn't *love* me.

"Look, Skeeter."

I was Skeeter again. I did not want to be a Kathryn.

"Look at the river out there. I love it. Loved it all my life. Practically lived on it when I was a kid. I don't *own* that river. Nobody does—or maybe everybody does. Either way. I don't *need* to own that river in order to *love* it. Same holds with people. You don't own people . . . to love them. Needing is . . . needing someone is begging for ownership."

"Is that the way it works? For everybody?"

"For everybody."

"You and Mom?"

"For me and your mother too. I think your mother and I had those two things mixed up for years. Needing,

42

instead of loving. When we found out we didn't own each other, that we didn't really want to . . . I don't make sense to you, Skeeter, I know. But could you believe your mother and I probably care for and respect each other more now than we ever have? I guess, Skeeter, you'd have to say it was a shaky marriage—but a strong family."

We crossed another fence and were in the city park.

I was going to ask him why he was leaving Dinty and me, but I didn't. Even my little girl voice couldn't have managed that.

The tennis courts were dark and empty as we circled behind the mesh backdrops and started up Croll's Alley.

"Could I come and visit you on weekends?"

He hugged me to him. "Of course. Come down and take my calls. Help in the lab. It's not that far. Ride Denver down. Plenty of places to stop and rest along the way. Sound like fun?"

"Yeah." And it did. It made more sense than training Denver to dodge barrels.

"You're going back tonight."

"Got to, Skeeter. Some things to check out first thing in the morning. I'll be back in the afternoon. Your mother wants me to look in on Thompson's mare."

It felt funny, having a part-time father. I slipped in the back door as Dad got into the pickup.

I wondered, though, as I climbed the dark stairs to my room, if I'd ever be able to separate my *love* for Dad from my *need* for him.

I turned on my TV to Channel 13. The late movie was *Death of a Salesman* with Lee J. Cobb. I switched it off. I was already watching the death of a family.

Chapter Six

THE ONLY GROWN-UP THAT I LIKED AS MUCH AS JOAN Kendall was Sally Stevens, who taught English when I was in seventh grade. Everyone liked her, and that was about the only year I can remember when we learned things. Even Ralph Barrett learned, and he hardly ever came to school because even in seventh grade he was always getting suspended.

Miss Stevens had just graduated from college, so she was a big change from teachers like Mrs. Wherle in the fifth grade. I don't mean just because she was young, but if you didn't know her, you might think she was a senior in high school. She was friendly and everything, but she never tried to be buddies with us. I hate it when teachers try that. It's so phony. They're always two months behind in the words they use—like saying "treemendous," when the *in* word is "dyno."

Miss Stevens is who I learned about old movies from. She was crazy about them and knew all about the actors and even the directors. In one unit, for extra credit, we could do movie reviews but the picture had to have been made before 1955. I picked *Rebel Without a Cause* that had this neat actor called James Dean in it. But it was obvious that something terrible was going to happen to him, so I only watched the first half, and in my paper, I fixed up the ending the way I wanted it to be.

Instead of being mad, Miss Stevens gave me an A and told me she liked my story better than the real one. That's the kind of teacher she was.

She was only there one year, mostly because of Mr. Holms, the principal. He didn't like her because she was so young, I think, and because all the kids were crazy about her. He thought she let us get away with things. He was always in the hall, just outside our door, and sometimes he listened in over the loudspeaker system. One day he sneezed and we all heard and laughed, and I don't think he listened any more.

For a while, I thought I'd like to be an English teacher, but after I met Joan, I decided I'd rather be a coach.

Until Marti came home, Joan was the most important and exciting person in my world. More important than my mother or my father or Dinty. I didn't feel funny about it then and I don't now.

I loved her. I loved her so much I wanted to *be* her. But it never was what adults call a crush. That sounds like something made out of fruit and sugar and if you dumped it on someone, it would be so sticky the person probably wouldn't be able to move.

I started to love Joan the day I told Dinty about—the

day I went down to sign up for tennis lessons, and Joan was sitting, looking so clean and shiny and beautiful, taking our names and giving instructions.

When she suggested that I'd be better with private lessons, she did it in a way that didn't mean I'd been some kind of dum-dum for showing up with the rest of the kids. She made it a compliment but not too much so I'd be stuck-up or embarrassed. That's very hard to do.

We began lessons two days a week and she made me work hard. She yelled a lot, but after a while I didn't mind because she wasn't yelling at *me*; she was yelling at what I was doing. At first I did feel rotten as if I were doing dumb things on purpose, but she guessed how I felt and explained the difference between *who* someone is and *what* someone does.

Maybe one reason I loved Joan was that she wasn't my mother. It's hard to explain because, of course, I loved Mom, but a lot of times that summer Mom and I didn't have any fun together. I don't very much like being serious. I can do it for about five minutes and that's all. Dinty says I have the attention span of a four-year old. But that summer everybody in my family was serious.

Anyway, most of the time, when I was with Mom, I knew she was thinking about what was happening to our family. It was as if she wanted to explain something to me that she didn't quite understand herself. And I wanted to understand too, but I didn't want to talk about it. So a lot of the time, we went in circles. And switching back and forth between being Kate with Joan and being Katie with Mom made me feel like a yo-yo.

For instance, there was this one day. I'd had my lesson with Joan from two until four, and I'd finally learned how to make my backhand go where I wanted it to. Joan had even missed a couple of my returns, and that didn't happen very often.

Then we started fooling around, the way Marti and I did a lot of the time. Like every time I'd get ready to serve, I'd look across the net and Joan would be making a toothy face and holding her racket up so she looked like a mouse in a cage. It doesn't sound very funny, but it broke me up.

Or if she was serving, I'd stand on one leg and flap my arms and pretend to be a heron. That made her double fault twice. Finally we stopped and went over in the shade.

I was hot and sweaty and my shirt was soaked, but Joan looked as if she'd stepped out of a shower. I don't understand how some people can do that. Mom is that way too. Even if she's been out on somebody's farm working on an animal, she never looks messy. That can give a child an inferiority complex.

"Would you like a root beer?" Joan drank them the way Mom drank coffee. I must have brought her two million of them from the stand that summer. She never asked me to. I just sort of knew when she wanted one.

"Not right now, but thanks. Hey, you know what I was thinking?"

"That I should go to Forest Hills this fall?" It wasn't very clever, but it made her laugh. I could usually make her laugh. I don't think Mom had laughed since I came back from camp.

"Not quite. I was thinking you ought to try out for the high school tennis team next year."

At first I thought she was joking, but then I knew she wouldn't tease me about that. All at once I could see it. I have a terrific imagination. There I was in a nifty sweat suit with Dawson High printed across the back. I'd just finished winning the most important match of the season, and all the junior high kids were crowding around, asking me to sign their yearbooks.

"Do you think I could make it?" Sometimes I can be realistic.

"I don't know." Joan was always realistic. "But your game has improved and if you don't make it this year, you will next."

I rolled over on my back in the grass and grinned up at the sky. That was the best compliment she'd given me all summer. "I'm glad you're not my mother."

"*You're* glad? What would I do with a monster like you? Besides, I would have been about six years old when you were born."

"*Guinness Book of Records.*"

"That record I could do without. When's your friend Marti coming back?"

That was one of the reasons Joan was so neat. She remembered Marti's name. I'd told her a lot about Marti and the stuff we'd done in camp other summers. She'd laughed and said that Marti sounded like a good kid. She didn't say "lovely child."

"She's coming home in about a week. If she hasn't died of food poisoning. You know why they wouldn't put us in the same session?"

Joan stretched out on the grass beside me. "I thought they drew names or something."

"Nope. They did it on purpose. Because of last summer. See, every year when the session ends, there's this kind of show that us kids put on. Skits and stuff."

"Like *Varieties* at the University, I suppose."

"Maybe. Anyway, Marti and I wrote this skit that was full of all sorts of dirty jokes. Like 'she was only the girdlemaker's daughter, but she lived on the fat of the land'."

Joan could make gagging noises almost as well as Marti.

"Or 'she was only the publisher's girl friend, but she kept it between the covers.' Anyway, at camp what we do most is sew leather stuff or sew a bunch of beads together. And there's this counselor that we hate and we call her Skinny Butt and she's in charge of crafts."

Joan looked at me. "This has to be going somewhere."

"Well, see, that summer there was this joke going around. Of course, it was very juvenile and sort of dirty. 'Did you hear about the cross-eyed seamstress? She couldn't mend straight.' "

Joan laughed. She really did, and she was an adult.

"All the kids at camp had heard this joke. So in our skit, we changed it a little bit like, 'Did you hear about the cross-eyed counselor? She couldn't sew straight.' And everybody knew we meant Skinny Butt. And it knocked everybody out. All the kids. They laughed for five minutes, and none of the counselors could figure out why it was so funny. But Skinny Butt figured out that something was wrong, so she called Marti and me in and tried to find out, but we pretended we didn't understand all the laughing either. Just the same, they put us down for separate sessions this summer."

"Oh, Katie, you've got to admit it is a dumb joke. There's nothing funny about it. But I suppose I would have done the same thing when I was your age, if I'd thought of it."

"There was a lot funny about it then—when we were

twelve. But Marti says when a person gets older, she forgets."

Joan reached over and mussed up my hair more than it already was. Usually I hate anyone touching my head, and if Mom does, it's meant to smooth my hair down, not muss it up. But I didn't mind when Joan did it. "Well, *this* older person is going home to take a shower. See if you can stay out of trouble until our next lesson. Okay?"

Just about anything in the world Joan said was okay with me.

The yo-yo business I was talking about happened that evening. I fixed dinner. I'd already taken care of Denver and had kind of planned on watching the early show on TV while Mom took her turn with the dishes.

It wasn't that I wanted to watch the movie; I just didn't know what else to do with myself. But before I could leave the kitchen, Mom stopped me.

"It's a lovely evening, Katie. Let's sit outside for a while and watch the sun set."

Mom has this really great voice—husky and sort of personal, even when she's talking on the telephone. It works with animals too. She was asking me for something. Not like, "Will you please pick up your room?" or "Would you like to go shopping for some new shorts?" She was asking me the same way Marti would ask if Marti ever had to. And that made me sad—that I hadn't thought of it first and made a present of it. You can make presents out of things like first stars and sunsets.

I'd done that once with Mother. It was kind of crazy, but it felt right. Earlier in the spring one afternoon, I'd walked past the florist on my way home from school. I had a dollar and some change in my pocket, and I'd meant to buy a new notebook. But somehow, I started thinking about Mom. How her face looked, her eyes especially.

It wasn't Mother's Day or anything, but I began thinking how hard she worked, and how we all depended on her, even Dad, and that though we all shared the chores around the house, there ought to be something more.

So I went in and bought her the two most beautiful roses—one yellow and one red. Mr. Ferris wrapped them in green paper, and I carried them home very carefully and left them on the kitchen table. I didn't put a card with them because I didn't know what to say.

I don't think I'll ever forget the way she unwrapped them. I mean there are a bunch of dumb songs about your heart in your throat, or your heart standing still, but that's how I felt while I watched her. I know that in all my thirteen years I never loved anybody as much as I loved her. And, at the same time, I felt awful. Why should such a little thing that just happened by accident mean so much to her?

At first she didn't say anything, and that was okay. Then she reached over and put her hand on my arm. It sounds crazy, but it was like she was seeing me and touching me for the first time. The only thing she said was, "My Katie."

And that's how she sounded when she asked me to go see the sun set.

We didn't talk at first. We just sat and looked at the colors of the evening. I began to feel awful. I smelled hamburgers cooking on somebody's grill. The locusts were buzzing in the trees. Denver nickered from the barn. It

51

was like so many other summer evenings, except then we'd all been together on the back porch. I felt homesick, and I wasn't even away from home.

Mom put down her empty coffee cup and turned to me.

"Katie. Your father and I sign the papers next week. I want you to know about it and I want to try to explain why all of this happened."

I didn't want to hear. There was something terrible about the sound of "signing papers." By writing down their names, they were erasing *me* . . . and Dinty. I wrapped my arms around myself and tried to choke off the empty feeling inside.

"Honey, I know how hard this is for you. But it *has* to be. You must know . . . you must understand how much your father and I love you and Dinty. That's one thing that won't ever change."

"You stopped loving each other."

She sighed deep in her throat. "Katie, your father and I still care about each other and that's one reason all of this is happening now. Sometimes loving means letting go while both people are still whole."

All I could think of was a movie I'd seen about these people in a lifeboat and there were other people hanging onto the side, and one by one they'd let go.

"But why did it have to be?"

"Because your father and I changed. Changed in different ways. The only thing that's stayed the same is how we feel about you."

The emptiness kept growing. "Why did you have to change? Why couldn't everything stay like it was?"

"We tried, Katie. For a while we really thought if we tried hard enough we could go back to where we'd been, who we'd been before. And you know what happened. When we weren't angry with each other, we were simply trying to be polite."

I knew Mom was telling me the truth, and for a while I hated my father. If he'd been stronger or smarter or something, he could have kept it from happening. It had to have been his fault. After all he *was* the father.

"But, Mom, everything is going to be so different." The hollowness had moved up into my throat.

"Remember my telling you once that breaking a pattern is hard. And different doesn't necessarily mean worse." She reached over and touched me on the cheek.

That's when I felt like crying, but I didn't because the next thing I knew was I felt like the mother and she felt like my daughter. I know it sounds funny, but I wanted to reach out and smooth her hair and tell her everything would be all right.

So I did what I always do when I feel creepy. I made what Marti calls one of my "lame-brain" remarks.

"Why don't you run upstairs and go to bed. You'll feel better in the morning."

Mom recognized the direct quote as her own and half laughed, "Oh Katie. Sometimes I don't know about you."

But what Mom didn't recognize was that I didn't know about me either.

Chapter Seven

ANYONE WHO HAS EVER SEEN AN ACTOR CALLED WALTER Brennan—he was with Humphrey Bogart in *Treasure of Sierra Madre*—would know exactly what Walt Seiffert looked like. They're both grizzly and old and they don't move very fast. Walt said if he had his way, he probably wouldn't move much at all.

I'd known Walt and Neva all my life, and for a while when I was small, I thought they were my grandparents. They lived on a farm south of town and we always bought eggs from them.

Whenever we drove into their driveway, the wheels of the pickup hardly stopped turning before Neva dashed out of the house. And then Walt would come around the corner of the barn and he always said the same thing: "I'm coming—coming a-running, but not very fast."

Nobody but Walt thought it was funny, but Dad always laughed as if he were hearing it for the first time. I learned to laugh too.

I had seen Marjorie Main once in *Ma and Pa Kettle*. I didn't watch the whole picture because it was too silly, but Neva could be a double for Marjorie Main. Neva was a big woman and even when she was standing still it was as if she were moving because there were always wisps of things sticking out. Her white hair never stayed smooth and threads hung out of the seams on her dress. She looked rumpled—and comfortable.

She sold things door to door—vanilla, cooking spices, shampoo—stuff she carried around in two suitcases that filled the trunk of her old red Buick.

Anyway, it was Walt and Neva who I decided to go and see the morning I didn't get to go into the city with Mom.

Mom needed some supplies for the clinic and had promised there'd be time to look at rackets at Olson's Sports. I wanted to see a T-2000 Steelie and I wanted to try a Smasher III, too. That's what Joan had, but it cost a bundle and I didn't know if I could talk Mom into buying one.

Mom left the house that morning looking really nifty in her yellow pants suit and white sandals. She was going to check on things at the clinic while I got dressed.

I was stepping into my new denim skirt when the phone rang.

"Katie?"

Why do people always ask who you are when they know you're the only one there?

"We're in the most unbelievable mess down here." It was Mom's Dr. Warner voice. "I can't possibly get away today."

"But Moth-ther." Sometimes even I can't stand the way I sound.

"I'm sorry, Katie, but it can't be helped. You do understand, don't you?"

"Yes." But I made sure that there was room for doubt.

She went on explaining about the mess at the office.

And I knew the yellow pants suit would hang in the closet at the office until one night Mom would come home bringing it and two or three other outfits, set aside along with the dinner party she'd missed, the country club picnic, and now, our trip. She had so much stuff down there she could have had a garage sale.

"It's okay," I said and hung up the phone.

What was there to do?

"Dial M for Murder," I heard one of my voices snarl.

I slouched down in the easy chair and for five minutes waited for the phone to ring again. It didn't.

I went to my room and took off the denim skirt and pulled on my Levis. They smelled horsey. "Gamey," Dad would have said.

And that's when I thought of Walt and Neva. They lived about ten miles from town, more than halfway to Hanway. I'd ridden out there lots of times before. Today, I'd ride Denver down and see Dad and stop at their place on the way.

I picked out a story for the ride. I decided to be Ann Blyth, whose happiness is ruined when she finds out she's adopted. I think it was *Our Very Own* or something like that.

Maybe I was adopted. And they hadn't told me. Marti asked me once if I hadn't noticed that there were twice as many pictures of Dinty in Mom's photo album as there were of me. So I *could* be leaving home to search for my real mother and father. The movie ended fine because her real mother wasn't half as nice as her adopted one.

There weren't many people driving the river road. One truck went past in a cloud of dust and gave a friendly honk. Most everyone around knew me. Not my name, maybe, but that I was Doc Warner's girl, and it didn't make any difference whether they meant my mother or my father.

It was nice to have people wave and honk on a beautiful morning with every leaf motionless as if someone had switched off the movie camera and frozen the frame.

I began to wonder if Walt or Neva would be home. Neva was probably out on her route. I suppose that in some ways it was funny of me to want to see them. After what was happening to Mom and Dad, I mean. Neva and Walt together weren't like any movie I'd ever seen. I sometimes wondered what their horoscopes said the day they got married.

A lot of the time they spent yelling at each other and for a while I'd thought they were really serious. Neva talked about how lazy Walt was—always in front of him, of course. When I thought about it I knew that must be one of the rules of *their* game. And he'd act like he was scared to death of her and then make a great fuss over starting to do something that hardly ever got finished.

And I never had heard them call each other "honey" or "darling," the way my folks used to; but on the other hand, *they* weren't getting a divorce.

Denver's coat was damp by the time we turned into

Walt's lane, shoulder-high with sunflowers and sumac. Puffs of dust blew up as we headed for the water trough by the empty hog house.

Walt was leaning back in a chair on the porch, his cap pulled down over his eyes. That was a sure sign that Neva wasn't home. Otherwise, he would have been down in the barn pretending to work.

I yelled hello.

He swung his feet off the porch rail and brought the old chair down with a crack that made Denver jerk his head up from the trough. "Hi there, Kateykins. Where ya off to?"

"Going to see Dad at Hanway." I wasn't sure if he knew about Mom and Dad or not.

"Down to Hanway, huh. Well, you're about halfway there." Walt sauntered down from the porch, hitching up his dirty work pants so the waistband formed a half moon beneath his belly. "Your . . . uh . . . your dad staying down these days?"

"Yeah." I pulled a cockle burr out of Denver's tail.

"Hear your dad bought the guy out."

"Yeah. Dinty's there helping him get squared away."

Why couldn't I come out and tell Walt the truth? That Dad had moved out. That Mom and Dinty and I were left with the house and the pet clinic.

"Don't let that horse get too much water. He'll founder in this kind of weather. Why don't you tie him down by the barn? And I'll get some buttermilk for you. Neva churned this morning."

I tied Denver and walked stiff-legged up toward the house and lay down in the long grass. Walt thought mowing a lawn a waste of time. It felt good to rest. I rolled over and looked at the sky.

Walt soon came shuffling down from the house balancing two glasses.

"Where's your buddy? What's her name? Marti?"

"Still at camp."

He handed me a glass and squatted down, leaning his back against a tree trunk.

"Things a little rough, are they?"

And I knew he was not talking about the ride. There were no starts to Walt's conversations. Mom would circle a subject, and Dad would hem and haw and tease and joke before he got down to being serious, but Walt went straight for the heart.

I nodded my head and gulped the buttermilk.

"There's worse things."

"Name one." The buttermilk was thick and lumpy.

"Lumbago."

"I don't even know what that is."

"Well, I'll have to try again." He paused as if he were shuffling a deck of cards. "I can think of one thing that's worse. Worse even than lumbago. That's to give up. Let things drift."

"Why's that worse?"

"When you're drifting, you're dead. Ever see a fish, floating two or three inches under the water? Either about done for or else he's already dead. Live one . . . and you've been fishing enough with your dad—the place to catch the live ones is where they're swimming upstream."

"Fish aren't people."

"Maybe not. Not so sure, though. No drifters, your mom and dad. Wouldn't go so far as to judge a corporation 'less I was part of it, but appears to me that if they decide splitting is right, then I got to believe it is."

"Kids should be able to pick their own parents."

"Your dad's a fine man. And there ain't a nicer woman nor a prettier one in the whole county than your mom. Every bit as good a vet as your dad. Helped me with lambing last spring. Why we worked together almost one whole night and through to the next morning. Has a way about her. Makes a man, even a fat old duffer like me, feel ten feet tall." Walt took off his stained cap and held it arm's length above his head.

For Walt it was a long speech, but then Neva wasn't around to cut him off. I waited, sipping the buttermilk, but the silence got long and I blurted out, "I'm never going to get married."

"Maybe you won't need to." He laughed and patted my shoulder with his big hand. "Maybe they'll outlaw marriage by the time you're ready."

"I'm not ever going to have kids, either."

"Kids are temporary. Have them eighteen years, if you're lucky and they leave. You've had thirteen years of that eighteen. Only five years short. Ain't bad."

"I suppose not."

"Look at it this way. You'll be leaving home one of these days. Off to college or something. Moving out on your family. Cause it sort of sounds that's what you're thinking your folks are doing on you."

"But that's different. They're doing it first."

"So what? Look at us here, for a minute. Take this buttermilk. Good, wasn't it? Drinking it out here under the tree? Both of us had to pay a price. It didn't come free. You had to ride nearly nine or ten miles on Denver, and I'll bet you got a sore butt to prove it. Me? Had to listen to Neva complain all the time she was pumping that churn this morning. Paid the price. Both of us. Worth it, wasn't it?"

I had to agree, even when I added the extra price, missing the trip with Mom and not getting my racket. Yes, I'd paid.

I drank the rest of the milk and handed the glass back to Walt.

"Yep, girl. Price tag on everything. You get what you pay for. Looks like you're getting short-changed sometimes. All evens out in the end, though." He yawned and stretched. "Well, girlie. Better hop to it. Promised Neva I'd clean out the hen house. Best to get done what she orders."

I walked down to the barn, but I wished I could have stayed the rest of the day with Walt, because we'd been talking about the divorce and yet neither one of us had said the word.

"Hang in there, girl." Walt hadn't stirred from under the tree. "Reading the other day where this fella said there was one thing gave him hope. Know what he said? Said, 'You never step in the same river twice.' Means you don't have to pay the same price twice. Something to chew on."

I guided Denver down the lane. Walt was still lying under the tree.

I thought about what Walt had said as I rode the last few miles to Hanway—about rivers and drifting dead fish and about change. But I didn't want things to change. I wanted them to stay the way they were before the bad stuff began.

Dad's pickup wasn't around when I rode up, but Dinty was out behind the office burning trash, and the look of surprise on his face was worth the sixteen-mile ride.

Just then Dad's truck careened down the street. He leaned out of the window as he wheeled into the parking lot.

"Well, look who's here. Skeeter."

"A dead Skeeter," I yelled back.

"You mean to tell me you rode all the way down?" He turned off the ignition and the motor chugged to a stop.

"Every mile and I'm still glued to the saddle. You didn't tell me it was so far."

He chuckled. "You didn't make it in one fell swoop, did you?"

"Nope. I stopped off at Walt's."

"You did, huh? Neva home?"

"No. Just Walt."

He climbed down from the cab and held Denver while I slid out of the saddle. "And what was our barnyard philosopher up to today?"

"Not much. We just talked . . . about fish . . . and a river . . . and corporations."

Chapter Eight

C OME ON IN AND SEE THE OFFICE, SKEETER." DAD SLUNG A coil of rope around his shoulder and grabbed his leather case. "Dinty. Drive the truck around and unload, will you?"

I followed Dad through the glass doors and into the reception room. It could have been a medical doctor's office except for the barking coming from the back room.

"Pretty fancy down here, isn't it?" Dad strode on ahead.

A woman was sitting on a swivel stool in front of a filing cabinet, her back to the door.

"And this is Florry," Dad grabbed the stool and swung the woman around. "Florry came with the business."

She wasn't much older than Joan and her blonde hair was swept into a rakish bun on top her head. I hated her on sight.

"This is Skeeter. She rode down today to look us over."

I hated the "us."

"Hi, Skitter. What do you think of it?"

"Great. Just great," I mumbled. What right did she have to call me Skeeter? Besides she couldn't even pronounce it.

All the time Dad was standing there grinning as if he'd done some kind of magic trick.

"But see what you've made me do," Florry pouted. "Honestly, Doc, you've made a mess of my cards." She dragged her eyes away from Dad and turned back to me. "You know, Skitter, it's a wonder we get anything done down here."

Dad chuckled like an eighth grader and rummaged in a desk drawer. "Come see the master suite, Skeet." He whirled a set of keys around his finger as his eyes moved from Florry to me and back again.

I was happy to follow him through the door and down the hall.

"See you around, Skitter," Florry called after us.

I pretended not to hear.

"This is really a great set-up, Skeeter." Did he sound phony! Like Robert Young in *Father Knows Best*, when one of his kids has done something really dumb. Dad was trying, though, trying to be the same old Dad—jolly and relaxed, but it wasn't working. I felt a little sick, but maybe that was because I hadn't had anything to eat since breakfast except Neva's buttermilk.

"Here we are, madam, the boss's suite." Dad bowed an exaggerated welcome as if he were a Sheraton bellhop.

I walked in slowly while Dad hurried to the windows and opened the drapes. I almost reached in my pocket for a tip.

Everything in the room was wrong. The pieces of furniture belonged at home, not in this place. The old walnut stereo from the rec room—I hadn't even noticed it was gone. Dad's Strato-lounger, the bowling trophies, the chair that Dinty and I used to turn upside down and call our horse—they were all there.

I looked into the bedroom. It was filled with stuff from our guest room. On the dresser top, Dinty's picture was at one end and mine at the other. Mom's picture was not there. And a double bed . . .

"Make yourself comfortable, Skeet. I've got some things to do. Thirsty? We've got a pop machine out back."

"I'll get some later." I hoped he didn't notice that my voice sounded funny.

I sprawled in Dad's chair and closed my eyes. I felt as if someone were sawing me in half: part of me wanted to be here with the familiar furniture and the other part of me wanted to run to the things that were left at home. I tried to imagine Dad alone here at night, but I kept seeing Florry's face instead.

"Say, girl," Dad filled the doorway again. "Just took a look at Denver. We ought to trim those hooves."

"Yea, I know. I was going to ask you before the barrel races. Forgot, I guess."

I felt him looking at me and I sank deeper into the chair.

"I suppose." He was being phony again. "Why not leave Denver down here with me? I can't get to him today, but he should be tended to. Dinty can take you back in the pickup. He wants to get some things from home anyway. That all right with you?"

"Sure." I sounded phonier than he.

"Okay. I'll tell Dinty. He'll have to get some gas before you leave. I've got to run now, but I'll be up Saturday. Oh, I forgot. Tennis going all right?"

But he didn't wait for my answer.

I sat alone and looked around the room. Nothing fit or matched. A cross between a rec room and a garage sale. Mom would have collapsed if she'd seen it. No, that was wrong. Mom never collapsed.

Before that summer she would have laughed. Once, to tease Dad, she had hung a horse-collar mirror over the Danish modern dresser. He didn't even notice, and when Mom pointed it out, he just blushed and said, "Well, it's a mirror, isn't it? Who cares how it looks? It's paid for."

I couldn't sit there any longer imagining things that weren't ever going to happen again. If I stayed, I knew I'd start crying, and I wasn't sure I could stop. I took one last look and tiptoed out and closed the door. The last thing I saw was Dad's chair. It looked out of place and alone and empty.

The muffler on the pickup needed fixing. If we wanted to talk, we had to yell at each other. But that was okay because a conversation with Dinty was like sharpening a knife. Everytime I said anything, I always got a sharper edge back. I decided he was like Dad. Dinty didn't think there was any point to talking unless you could laugh at the same time. "If you can't laugh, cut out."

Mom did agree once, only she quoted from some book. She could always back up what she said.

"There's a better translation of the same idea, Dinty. *When the sorrows of life encompass you, tell it to your salad bowl and go forth singing* . . . or something like that. I can find the exact quote if you wish."

Dinty never wished.

"Well, what'd you think of Dad's pad?" Dinty steered the pickup onto the river road.

"Early-America Awful."

Dinty let up on the gas and leaned forward against the steering wheel. "Not bad. Not bad. That'll do for the phylum."

He'd taken Biology II last year in school and it had opened up a whole new language for him. He still didn't know much about biology, though.

"Now for the classification under phylum, I'd have to say . . . ah . . . Bachelor Bare . . . or maybe . . . How about Modern Separation Salvage?"

I laughed even if I didn't want to. And then I asked him what I'd been thinking all afternoon. "Do you think he's really happy, Dinty?"

"Happy? I don't think he knows when he is happy and when he's not. He never thinks about it. Another day. Another dog . . . or hog . . . sick. Sick dog. Sick hog. Not sick Dad. After all, he's a doctor."

I guess somehow over that summer I'd forgotten that there were times when I really did like Dinty.

"How were we so lucky to get not one, but two doctors for parents?"

"Planned parenthood. Just think. They could have

been teachers. Can you imagine having Mrs. Wherle for your mother?"

"But we could have had a regular father who went to work at eight and came home at five and a mother who stood behind a picket fence and wore aprons. Remember Dick and Jane? And Spot and Puff in first grade?"

"I'm getting carsick." Dinty grabbed his stomach.

"They made it look so simple, didn't they?"

"They *were* simple. 'Life is real. Life is earnest.' "

"Garbage." I had a better word, but I decided not to shock him.

"I had to read that poem in seventh grade once. 'Life is real, life is earnest.' And I wrote, right in the library book with a ball point, *'Earnest who?'* Got caught and had to stay after school for three nights in a row."

"You never told me." It had never occurred to me that Dinty might have a secret life.

"Lots of things I don't tell. Some things are my own business and nobody has a right to them. You're the same way. Dad's a little like that, but you can't see it quite as much. Of course Mom is. Very, very private. You've got to admire her. She's the original Wonder Woman. Magic bracelets, secret power, and all."

I wanted him to be serious. "It's so awful, Dinty. What are we going to do?"

"Nothing *to* do. It's like mumps. You wait until the swelling goes. Once you've had mumps you don't get them again." Dinty kept looking out the side window; then he looked over at me. "Hey. You're crying."

"Well, dammit! Why aren't *you* crying?"

"*I can't.* And watch your language. None of that locker room talk. Sound familiar?"

"Sounds familiar." And I swallowed the sob before Dinty noticed.

The tires on the pickup whined through the loose gravel as a stock truck full of feeder cattle swooshed by. The duals shot out pebbles that hit the windshield and rattled down on the fenders like hail.

Dinty worked the pickup back into the smoother track and broke out in his awful tenor:

> "Puuuleeese releeeeese me,
> Let mee gooooooooooooooo.
> I don't looooove yew ennny moooore."

"Oh, knock it off, Dint."

"Just trying to cheer you up."

"I'd rather listen to a sick cow."

"Okay. Okay. But turn off the waterworks."

"I know. 'Go up to your room if you're going to sit there sniffling.' End of quote. Wonder Woman."

"That's what I've been trying to tell you, dummy. Go to your room. Figure it out for yourself. Let go! It's over. Then the hell with it. It's not the end of the world. Quite."

"Watch your language. Remember Mom's soap treatment?"

"I remember. But you remember a few things too. Take care of Kate." He paused as he turned sharply onto the side street. "I'll ride Denver back for you when Dad gets done with him. It'll give me a chance to check up on a new Kate. See if she's ready to break out of the Dick and Jane world." He grinned at me. "You know, you'd make a lousy Jane."

Dinty steered the pickup into our drive, a little too fast if Mom had been home to see, braked to a stop, and jumped out to open the door for me.

Mom didn't ask much about my visit to Dad at Hanway, and I was glad. I didn't want to be an undercover agent for either one of them.

But that night, before I went to bed, I dug out the beaded ring I'd made in camp and mailed it to Dad the next day.

Chapter Nine

ONE OF THE HARDEST THINGS THAT SUMMER ABOUT LIVING in Dawson and having my parents get a divorce was making up excuses for Dad's staying at Hanway. Sometimes it would be some of Mom's friends I'd run into down at the grocery store or some of the kids that were still around who would start firing the questions at me. I finally decided that just because people asked me questions it didn't mean I had to answer them. So I stayed by myself as much as possible, and when I had to be at the tennis courts, I latched onto Joan for protection.

I soon ran out of excuses—excuses like, "He's taking a refresher course this week at the University" or "All his equipment is down at the new office" or "He's so busy at Hanway." But I'm sure no one was fooled; after all, the neighbors knew how seldom the pickup was parked in our drive anymore.

I guess Buffi Peterson was the worst of the kids. It was

a hot July day and I broke my rule about keeping to myself and decided to go down to the pool for a swim. It was a mistake. Buffi was there in a new bikini. I was sitting on the edge of the pool, dangling my feet in the water, when she came over—to show off her suit, I think.

"There's a swim meet tonight. Your folks coming? Dinty's on the team."

I hadn't paid enough attention to what Dinty had been doing afternoons when he wasn't helping Mom or down at Hanway to answer, but I grunted, "I dunno."

"How come Dinty's never around? Doesn't he live with you and your Mom anymore?"

"Of course. Where'd you get such a dumb idea? He has to help Dad a lot of the time with the new office."

"Oh, really." Buffi readjusted her bikini top. "Does your dad stay down there all the time?"

"Not all the time." And I wasn't quite lying—but almost.

"You should tell your folks about the meet. Suppose they'll come? I got to sell four more tickets."

"I'll ask them."

"When'll you see them? To find out for sure? I got to turn in my money by six thirty."

"They'll be home for dinner . . . I think. Unless they have a late call."

"How about you calling me about six? I'll save two tickets for them."

I knew I was cornered. At six, I'd be in the same spot, trying to make up some excuse. So, without thinking, I said, "They'll take two tickets, I know. Give them to me. I'll bring you the money. I'll bring it over to your house by six." I took the tickets, stuck them under my towel, and slipped into the water and swam out to the deep end. I knew Buffi couldn't follow me there.

I paid for the tickets myself—out of what was left from my allowance and the check I'd written from Mom for my tennis lessons.

Nobody used them.

It was that way all that summer. I felt completely boxed in. I couldn't talk to anyone without lying. Mom didn't want to talk (and neither did I) and Dad was gone. There were times when I felt absolutely desperate because if I did talk to someone, it all led up, some way, to the divorce. And I couldn't write to Marti.

Before I went off to camp, after Marti and I first found out we wouldn't be going to the same session, we decided we wouldn't write to each other. "It's too bourgeois," Marti said. "We'll communicate by ESP." Marti had been reading up on Extra Sensory Perception—and French.

I, of course, agreed to try ESP.

"It'll save stamps," Marti argued, "and time. And paper. And envelopes."

I was easy to convince when Marti argued.

So before I left for camp we set the contact time for 8:17 to 8:43. That was Marti's idea too. But when I was at camp, we had our nightly "get-togethers" around the campfire from eight on. And when I got home from camp, I could never concentrate the way Marti said a person should, because I was always thinking about Mom and Dad and the divorce.

Not that I didn't try. I'd go up to my room at exactly 8:17, sit cross-legged in the middle of the floor, and attempt to "empty my mind," but I could never last. My legs would start to ache and my back would itch. For the first ten minutes I was supposed to repeat Marti's name over and over as I breathed. After ten minutes of that, I was to send my message. The last ten minutes I was to sit and wait for Marti's message.

I didn't get any.

One night, I was really feeling down, I gave in and started a real, honest-cross-your-heart letter to Marti. And then I found I was looking forward to going up to my room every night at eight o'clock and writing another part to the letter. It wasn't long before I had several pages. But somehow, I could never quite bring myself to end the letter because I'd think maybe I'd want to add something to it the next night.

Tuesday

Dear Marti,

It's a long summer.

A get-up-go-to-bed summer with nothing in between. I play tennis, ride Denver, swim sometimes. I'm a walking, talking zombie.

It's all because of what happened after I got back from camp.

~~Dinty met me~~

~~I got off the bus~~

~~It all started~~

Friday

Dear Marti,

Do you know you can listen so hard you can make your ears ache? Really ache? It feels like the insides of your ears are being stretched. I suppose it's like eyestrain. Ear strain.

74

Did you get in Indian Village this year or are you still stuck in Deer Hollow? I would have made it but we got the Dirty Rag Award for our tent three days in a row. It wasn't my fault, either.

~~I was reading this column in the newspaper~~
~~I have been reading a lot of books lately about~~

Sunday Night

Dear Marti,
I think I am suffering from an advanced case of rigor mortis. I do things but they aren't any fun. I am thinking of painting a three-inch red grin on my face, gold-plating my hair, and going out trick-and-treating. I've been watching Denver out in the lot. He has a set schedule. He moves around according to the hour of the day. In the morning he's behind the barn. By noon he's inside. The afternoons he spends under the willow and at night he's up by the gate asking to be petted.
Maybe at night, he gets lonely for the day.

Tuesday

Dear Marti,
There was a real old movie on last night with Katherine Hepburn. It was called *A Bill of Divorcement*. I didn't watch.

Wednesday

Dear Marti,
I've been reading a lot lately. I found this way to find your character by numbers. You write out your first and last name and then there's a chart

with a number for each letter. You number each
letter and add them up and keep adding until it's
one number. Then this chart tells you what you
are like.

I did one for you and one for me. This is yours.
Your number is *two*.

*Two is a gentle perceptive number symbolic of
helpfulness and diplomacy. Associated with the
moon, it is constant, yet ever-changing.*

Mine came out to *six*.

*Six symbolizes harmony, beauty, balance, and
rhythm. The planet Venus holds sway over this,
the most stable of all vibrations.*

I think yours fits. I don't think mine does.

Saturday Night

Dear Marti,

Dinty's at a swim meet. Mom's over at Laura
Dobbs. Dad is in Hanway, and I am alone. Really
alone. Alone alone. I want something but I don't
know what. I've been to the refrigerator twice, but
nothing looks good. But I'm hungry just the same.

I did a terrible juvenile thing last night. I couldn't
sleep. So I got mad and started punching my pil-
low, as hard as I could, like a boxer. Then I yelled
(not loud enough for anyone to hear), "I hate
you! I hate you!" with every punch.

I felt better after I'd done that, and I finally went
to sleep and slept until nine this morning. I didn't
even hear Mom leave for work.

Tuesday
Dear Marti,
I've got something to tell you before someone else does.

Wednesday
Dear Marti,
My folks are getting a divorce.

Thursday
Dear Marti,
Divorce means to *get rid of*. I looked it up in the dictionary.
But if the party of the first part wants "to get rid of" the party of the second part, what is the party of the third part supposed to do if the party of the third part doesn't want to "get rid of" any one?

Friday
Dear Marti,
I was playing our game of "What If?" last night, but it wasn't any fun, alone. All I could think of were the wrong questions.
What if Dad marries again and I get a stepmother? What if Mom marries again and I get a stepfather? Or a stepbrother? Or a stepsister? Or a half-brother? Or a half-sister? Are there step grandfathers?

But I never sent the letters to Marti.

Chapter Ten

I DECIDED, AFTER WATCHING ROSALIND RUSSELL IN A MOVIE called *His Girl Friday*, to chalk up some brownie points with Mom by taking charge of the mail. I was still hoping she'd buy me a new metal racket, and I figured that going to the post office, forwarding Dad's mail, and sorting out the letters from the bills might help me get it.

That's why I was the one to see Grandfather's card that afternoon:

Dear Helen,
Arriving Wednesday at four. John and Hazel went fishing in Canada, so I'll visit you first and then go on to Vernon's.

Father

It *was* Wednesday. It *was* 1:30. I had a tennis lesson at two. He'd be here in three hours.

What could I do in three hours to glue the family together for three days? Grandfather always stayed exactly three days.

In movies, if there was a grandfather in the picture, kids always called him Pops or Gramps or Grandad and fell all over themselves when he came to visit. And he'd always be played by someone who looked like Edmund Gwynn— the Santa Claus in *Miracle on 34th Street*.

Not my grandfather. Dinty and I had to practically stand at attention when he arrived, and after about three minutes he'd have the whole house operating on his schedule: breakfast at seven, eggs sunny-side up, the portable TV in *his* bedroom.

I'd always been a little scared of him, though he'd never yelled at me or anything. He was taller than Dad, and his hair was thick and he had a little, trim mustache that didn't look grampish at all. It looked like it belonged to a banker and that was okay, I guess, because that's what he was.

When I was younger and went to Sunday school, I could never say, "Our Father who art in Heaven" without imagining Grandfather's face.

I sometimes thought Mom might be a little afraid of him too.

I tossed the rest of the mail on the kitchen table and ran for the phone. I didn't think the folks had told any of the relatives about what was going on.

Mom had left the office so I asked her assistant to have her call back.

I called the root beer stand in the park and asked them to tell Joan that I couldn't come for my lesson.

I looked around the house. It was a mess. I was supposed to have cleaned the day before, but I'd spent too much time down at the courts. Some days I sat through all Joan's lessons, from beginners on up; and some days she'd play me a game or two, just for fun, before she went home.

I don't mind cleaning the house when it's really awful —that way I can see where I've been. I washed the dishes piled in the sink, got out the vacuum and did the floors, made a fast tour with the dustcloth, and things looked pretty respectable.

Mom hadn't called.

I had to tell someone about Grandfather. I couldn't let him walk in on our new living arrangements. I wasn't sure where Dinty was. He'd said something about helping Walt out with his beans.

I put in a person-to-person call to Dad.

"Grandfather's coming. To visit. Today."

"Today!"

"In an hour."

"Where's your mother?"

"I couldn't get her. She was out."

"Listen, Skeeter." There was a long pause. "Can you manage till I get there? Take care of the old man some way. Show him the new fence. Run some barrels. I'll get hold of your mother."

"Okay. I've sort of cleaned up around here."

"Fine."

"Should I tell him anything?"

"No." Was Dad afraid too? "No. Just go on as if . . . as you usually do."

"Sure."

I still kept waiting for Mom to call. I even hoped Dinty would walk in.

I changed into clean shorts and my Camp Sacajawewa T-shirt and stood by the front window watching for Grandfather.

I'd never known my grandmother; she died before I was born. Of course, I'd seen pictures of her, but somehow that never made her real. Obviously she had existed; after all, there was Mom and her two brothers and they had to have come from somewhere. But I couldn't begin to imagine a grandmother sitting across from Grandfather at breakfast. Maybe if she were alive, I'd have felt more comfortable with him.

Grandfather never sounded comfortable talking to Dinty or me. He'd ask all the regular questions about school and sports and stuff, but they didn't seem natural. More as if he'd memorized some kind of list. Of course, there was only one other grandchild in the whole family besides us, and Grandfather only saw us once a year. Maybe he just didn't know how to act with kids our age.

I kept watching from the window and betting that he'd be in the next bunch of five cars that came down the street, but there weren't enough cars to make that interesting, so I changed the rules and counted the cars going up the street too.

Then I saw him, looking more like a judge in court than a banker. He was concentrating on turning his car into the exact center of our driveway.

I waited inside as he unlocked the car trunk, took out his suitcase, slammed the trunk shut, and marched up the front walk as if he were inspecting Dinty's last job of lawn mowing. Grandfather said you could tell people's characters by the way they kept up their lawns. Dinty's sidewalk fringes didn't show much character. Mine always did. I was a better mower than a duster.

I opened the door with a "Hello, Grandfather." I almost felt like doing a Shirley Temple curtsey and adding, "Colonel, sir."

He jumped a little. "I didn't think anybody was home."

"Mom's out on a call. And Dad . . . Dad's . . . I just talked to him on the phone."

He set his suitcase down in the middle of the living room. "Changed it around some, haven't you?"

I glanced around the room. It did look different with Dad's big leather lounger gone and his bowling trophies off the mantle.

"You didn't throw that good leather chair out, did you?"

Grandfather was a saver.

"No. We . . . we . . . moved it down to . . . we moved it."

"That was my favorite chair." He sat down in Mom's new bentwood rocker, his knees spread.

"Can I get you something to drink? Iced tea? Water? Or I can make some coffee?"

"Nothing. Nothing. I stopped up the road a piece." He continued to study the room.

"I can take your bags up."

"Sit still, girl. I don't have to be waited on. How's your folks and David?"

Grandfather refused to call him Dinty.

"Fine."

"You've grown since last year. You're going to be a

looker some day." He studied me as if I were part of the furniture.

"I don't know about that." I turned red and sat down on the far end of the sectional.

"You will be. Mark my word."

"Would you like to come out and see Denver? Dad put up a new fence for him."

"If you like. When do you expect your folks home?"

"Oh, anytime now. Let me call Mom again. Maybe she's back by now."

I escaped to the kitchen. But she wasn't back.

So I rode Denver for Grandfather and showed him the new fence and told him about Dinty's getting to start on the varsity track team last spring and told him about Dad's new practice in Hanway. I didn't tell him that Dad had moved out.

And Grandfather listened, nodding and stroking one corner of his mustache.

"Can we sit down now?" he motioned to the ground underneath the willow.

That nearly wiped me out. I mean I'd never imagined him sitting in the grass. I thought he'd been born wearing a suit and white shirt and necktie. Mom never let Dinty and me sprawl on the living room floor when Grandfather was visiting.

We both sat down, and while I watched he actually loosened his tie and undid the top button of his shirt.

"What else has been going on this summer, Kathryn?"

For a minute I was ready to blurt out the whole story, but then I caught myself and figured it was just another of those questions he'd memorized. So I repeated, for what must have the eight-millionth time, all the junk I'd done at camp. I really made mileage on my Camp Sacajawewa camp session that summer. I even threw in my tennis lessons with Joan to keep things going.

The funny part was that for the first time I could remember, he looked interested and I got more excited telling him about the tennis tournament at camp than I'd been when it was happening. But then it was also the first time in my life that I'd ever been alone with him for more than two minutes.

When I finally quit talking, he grinned at me. I don't mean smiled. I mean grinned. I didn't know he could do that either.

"Say, Kathryn. Look at this." He pulled up a blade of the wide-leafed grass, put it edgewise between his thumbs and blew a loud shrill whistle. "I can still do it. What do you think of that?"

I'd known how to do it ever since Dinty showed me when I was five, but Grandfather looked so pleased that I didn't want to hurt his feelings.

"How do you do that?"

"Here. I'll show you. It's a good thing to know."

I tried, then, and pretended it wouldn't work. "Guess I'll have to practice."

He looked at me and raised one eyebrow. I've never been able to do that. Marti and I had practiced for hours in front of my bedroom mirror, but both eyebrows always went up, not just one. We *had* learned to sneer—but we always ended up laughing instead of sneering.

"You're a fine horsewoman, Kathryn, but you're a terrible actress. And you're very polite to an old man."

Then he laughed, and the first thing I knew, I was

laughing too. That was almost the best I'd felt all summer.

When we stopped laughing, we sat for a while not saying anything, and it wasn't at all uncomfortable. Denver stood nearby pretending to ignore us, but his ears flicked so I knew he was listening.

"Did you mind very much, not going to Uncle John's house and having to come here instead?"

Every year that I could remember he'd done the same things at the same times, and we had always been Thanksgiving. I wondered if he liked seeing his children for just three days every year. It was sort of like what happens to some kids when their parents get divorced. It's called "visiting rights."

"No. I don't mind. That's one thing you learn, sooner or later. That children are people with plans and ideas of their own. They have their own special lives to live."

I nodded. That was what I was finding out about parents, too.

"Say, I noticed when I came, your dad's cannas are in bad shape. Need watering. That place in Hanway must be keeping him busy."

I nodded again. I didn't want to lie to him, but I didn't want to tell him the truth either.

"Well, why don't we go back up to the house? I could use a cup of tea now, and your folks will be home soon. Won't they?" He stood up, brushed himself off, buttoned his collar and tightened his tie. He looked like Grandfather again.

I followed him back to the house and got tea ready and sat drinking it with him at the kitchen table, and still Mom didn't call.

"You know, I get a letter from your mother once a

week. Regular as clockwork." He looked at me over the rim of his cup.

I hadn't known. I'd never paid any attention to my mother's letters and I guess I wouldn't have thought there was that much to write about anyway. Unless. . . .

"That's pretty good. She's so busy at the clinic and all."

"Every week. Of course they may not be very long. May not tell me everything." He pulled out his pipe and searched his pockets. "Must have forgotten my tobacco. Your dad still keep his in the den?"

"Sure. I'll go look. I think there's some there."

I hurried down the hall with my fingers crossed, and it worked. There was a tinfoil packet in the desk drawer.

Grandfather thanked me and started filling his pipe. I've never understood why anyone wants to smoke a pipe. It takes so long getting one ready and then there's all that puffing to get it lit.

But he didn't puff. He just felt the tobacco. "My God, Kathryn, how long has he had this around? It's be better in a fireplace than a pipe."

"I'm sorry. He must have the new pouch with him. He'll bring it when he comes."

The Leo horoscope that I'd chosen for that day had been right: "Quick action will avert domestic disaster."

He put down the pipe and leaned back in his chair. "You asked me about my visits. I want to explain something that I've found important. At least for me, and maybe for you sometime, too."

It sounded like a lecture coming up, but I remembered how he'd looked under the willow and tried to appear interested.

"Having your uncles and your mother leave home and build their own lives, losing your grandmother—well, all of those things were hard in different ways. How hard depends on how you handle it."

"Yes, Grandfather," I said and hoped I didn't sound like a parrot.

"It's like the way an oyster makes a pearl. Takes a grain of sand that burns and cuts its insides and lives with it. Goes about its clammy business, covers the sand over, and makes a pearl. Pearls are lovely when they come out perfectly formed. Or even if they're a little lopsided, for that matter."

"Yeah. Yes, I mean. It's like tennis, sort of. Practice and practice on my serve and that's not much fun. But Joan says sometime soon, it'll work right for me. That will be kind of like a pearl, won't it?"

He nodded and was about to say something when we heard the front door open.

For a minute it was like old times, and if I hadn't known differently, I would have thought it was real.

Mother was smiling and Dad was behind her, reaching for his pipe. Mom hugged Grandfather, and he kissed the top of her head. Then Dad stuck out his free hand and Grandfather shook it with, "You're looking prosperous, Vince."

"We're not doing too bad," Dad answered and stuck his pipe in his mouth.

Mom walked around behind me and put her hands on my shoulders. "Has Katie been taking care of you, Father? I'm sorry I was out, but we didn't know you were coming."

"I know. I know." Grandfather flicked an imaginary speck of lint from his trouser leg.

I was beginning to think being a grandfather was not the easiest thing in the world.

"I had a change in plans with John and Hazel taking off. But I'll go there for Thanksgiving—instead of coming here as we planned."

I heard the back door slam, and Dinty burst into the room. He didn't see Mom or me. Not even Grandfather at first. He saw only Dad.

"Dad! What are you doing here?" Then he saw Grandfather and his face slowly took on the shade of his hair.

What followed was like a bad movie. Dad tried to cover up and he was a worse actor than I. Mom jumped in with, "Well, of course your father is here." She didn't earn any Oscars with that one either.

Then Dinty, with his lame line, "I mean . . . I thought you had a meeting tonight, Dad."

And Dad made it even worse by answering, "Meeting? What meeting?"

It went on for what seemed forever, and it all sounded so phony. I couldn't look at Grandfather. Just when I thought I was going to have to make an excuse about feeding Denver, Grandfather finally had a chance to say something.

"Helen. Vincent. Now will you please stop it for a minute."

No one thought it was a question. They all stopped talking and looked first at each other and then at Grandfather and then at me.

"No. Kathryn hasn't told me anything. And there's no reason why she should have. But I haven't been a banker —and a father—all these years for nothing. I have eyes and good ears too."

I don't know if Dinty was holding his breath, but I was. I thought Grandfather was going to bawl them out just as if they were little kids. He didn't, and I was glad.

Dad and Mom said something at the same time so that nobody could understand a word. Dinty stole my excuse about taking care of Denver and left.

There wasn't much to stay for. Grandfather said he'd take us all out for dinner if we wanted to go, and Dad said he had to get back to Hanway, but that he'd be back the next day, and Mom said she'd love to be taken out for dinner, and so would I and probably Dinty too. She was right. If Dinty had been on the *Titanic*, he would have waited to eat dinner before the ship sank.

Grandfather stayed for the whole three days, but I didn't talk to him again. He spent one day with Dad down in the new office and the next day he spent with Mom at the clinic.

But when Grandfather left, he handed me a blade of grass and winked.

"Have you learned to whistle through this yet?"

And I grinned and said, "Sure. Don't you remember? You showed me how."

Chapter Eleven

MARTI'S BUS WAS OVER HALF AN HOUR LATE, AND I'D BEEN sitting on the curb waiting for almost forty-five minutes. There's not much of a view from a street corner in a small town. I'd tried walking around, looking in store windows, but they still had the same stuff in them that had been there at the beginning of the summer. They really didn't change anything; they'd just added a whole bunch of back-to-school stuff, which is very depressing to someone who has to go back to school.

So I sat on the curb and stared at the gutter, and that was depressing too. Nothing to see but a gum wrapper, some cigarette butts, and a chewed-up cigar.

But I thought about Marti and felt better. Every one needs a best friend. Marti had been mine since she moved to town four years earlier. Her folks had grown up in Dawson and then moved away for a long time to California. Of course they knew everybody in town when they came back, but Marti didn't, and she was lonesome at first. You know how it is when a new kid comes to school; everybody's afraid to make friends.

But I liked her the minute I saw her. She was shorter than I and about twice as big around. That didn't exactly help her fit in at first, either. She wasn't so much fat; she was round, like a little kid's drawing—all circles.

The first thing I thought when I saw her was that if she weren't so round she'd be beautiful. She had very blond hair that wasn't wavy like mine; it was smooth and slick and fell straight down so she could part it in the middle, the way they do in magazines. She had green eyes, really green, the way leaves are in summer. And her skin never tanned, even when she was out in the sun a lot.

One of the best things about her was that her birthday was the same day as mine, October 9. I found that out right away because if anyone new came to our homeroom, Mrs. Wherle—she was our homeroom teacher too—made them introduce themselves and tell practically a life history. So as soon as Marti sat down, I passed her a note and signed it "Soul Mate." Of course I wouldn't do that now, but four years ago I was only nine and didn't know any better.

Anyway, we did a lot of stuff together and it was never boring. Even after the other kids got to know her and like her, we were still best friends. She has a great sense of humor and can belch louder than anyone else in our class, even Swede Kramer.

The only thing was, I could never make her understand the advantage of picking the best horoscope prediction. She refused to be anything but a Libra. She has more character than I.

This was the first summer we hadn't gone to camp together and it felt really funny not to have her around. I guess that's why I was depressed. I should have been just plain happy. We'd always told each other pretty much everything. Except I hadn't said anything about the way things had been between Mom and Dad. And now they were getting a divorce.

See, divorces don't happen in small towns. Small towns are supposed to be like those Andy Hardy films with Mickey Rooney and Judy Garland where the story always ends with dancing and singing. None of my friends' parents were divorced, and as far as I knew, never had been. The closest was when Drusie Simms's father left, but he wasn't really her father, and he wasn't married to her mother, either.

Before I could think any more, the bus pulled in and kids started getting out. First came the littlest ones. Little kids always sit up front closest to the driver. They piled over each other in a hurry to get to the beaming mothers and fathers who had come to meet them.

Marti was the last one out. I looked at her and didn't even know her for a minute. The circles had disappeared. Her long blond hair was cut short. But the biggest surprise of all was *she had boobs*. I mean, the last time I saw her, her T-shirt had been almost as flat as mine.

It was crazy, but at first I was afraid to talk to her. I guess I thought her head might have changed as much as the rest of her. But then she looked at me and grinned and made a record belch so I knew it really was Marti.

"Welcome back to the pits, Lovely Child." I took her tennis racket while she dragged her duffel bag out of the pile beside the bus. "What happened to you in the wilds? Did they have you on bread and water?"

She crossed her eyes and made noises like throwing up. "Bread and water would be better than the junk they gave me. I forget every year how awful it is. And our folks actually pay for it. But the important part is, look what's grown."

"Yeah. If you stick them out any farther you won't be able to see where you're walking."

That knocked her out. And I knew for sure I loved Marti more than anyone else in the world.

We took our time going to her house. I pretended to be her mother, who is really a very nice person, but extra polite, even to Marti. I asked her all the dumb questions about summer camp that I knew her mother would ask, and called her "dear" at the end of every sentence. It's a game we play about parents or teachers. We call it RT—Rehearsal Test.

Marti can be my mother better than my own mother.

Anyway, she told me all the right answers about camp until we got almost to her front porch. Then she stopped and looked around very sneakily and whispered, even though there wasn't anyone within five blocks of us. "Old Skinny Butt Sybhorst got knocked up."

I dropped the tennis racket right on the sidewalk. Luckily it was in a press, so it didn't break.

"How?"

"I imagine the same way it always happens." Marti could also leer better than anyone; she learned by watching reruns of Groucho Marx shows.

Skinny Butt had been a counselor *every* summer we'd been at camp and everybody hated her. She had the biggest behind that we'd ever seen, but that wasn't why we didn't like her. I mean a person can't help how she looks. But she was always extra nasty about following rules and making us get to bed on time, and she pushed the little kids around. We used to spend at least three nights a week trying to think of how to get even with her.

"Yea, I know but how? And who would be that dumb?" I picked up the racket. "And how do you know? Did she tell everybody?"

Before Marti could answer, her mother came out the front door, and everything turned into a grand homecoming. I decided not to stick around, but Marti promised to come over that afternoon and tell me the whole story.

The way things turned out, though, we didn't get to see each other until the next day, because by the time I'd gotten through with my tennis lesson in the afternoon, Marti's folks had decided to go see friends in the city, and she had to go along. I knew if I were ever a parent, I'd never make my kids go anywhere with me. I even wrote that down in the book where I keep my rules for watching movies and the list of the best horoscopes for the month.

When we did get together again, we talked about Skinny Butt (it was the guy who picked up the camp garbage), about Marti's boobs (they were there all the time, but they didn't show until the circles went away), about whether as freshmen we ought to go out for the school paper (both of us are extremely literate).

And we talked about tennis. Even in her circular days, Marti had been pretty good. That summer she'd gotten better. She showed me the first-place trophy she'd won in the tournament during her session.

"Who ever heard of a leather trophy—a tooled leather tennis trophy?"

It really was dumb-looking—a flat piece of leather cut

out in the shape of a racket, but it was better than mine which was a lopsided tennis ball.

"You know, Sensitive Child, they're leather freaks at that place. If they could do it, they'd have leather bath towels."

"Or make us wear leather underwear."

"Or use leather toilet paper."

It was very childish, but a lot of fun.

Then I thought of something neat. "Why don't we both sign up for the town tennis tournament? It's next week, and that way we could collect real trophies."

Marti thought for a minute. That's one of the things I like about her too. She doesn't just open her mouth and answer. She considers ideas, which is quite adult and unusual for a thirteen year old. "Why, my dear, what a sterling idea."

She was being Mrs. Wherle, who was our guidance counselor in junior high after she got promoted from fifth grade classroom teacher. Everything was either "sterling" or "reprehensible" with Mrs. Wherle. It took us a long time to figure out how they were spelled so we could look them up and find out what they meant.

Then Marti had a second thought. "There's one thing, Sensitive Child. If we do that, we'll probably end up playing each other in the finals. One of us will have to lose."

I hadn't thought of that. I'd seen us as co-champions. "Yeah. But what we could do is, we could take turns with the trophies. You know, trade every month?"

"Sterling."

So we went to City Hall and signed up for the tournament. We also just missed getting our names in the paper . . . in the police column.

It was that same evening. Mom had to stay late at the clinic, and Dinty was still with Dad in Hanway, and Marti had three dollars left from camp. We decided to walk down and get something to eat at the Drive-In.

When we finished, we didn't want to go home. We didn't have enough money to go to the skating rink, and we sure didn't feel like watching kids drive around the town square. That is called "scooping the loop," and we both thought it was dumb because the same kids in the same cars drove around and around, honking and waving every time they met. The town cop didn't like it much either.

It's hard to find something fun to do in a small town, especially on long, hot August evenings. The only stuff on television was reruns from last winter or summer replacements that were dumber than the reruns. Besides, watching television can be dangerous to your mental health.

Marti and I wandered down to the park and sat on one of the benches and watched the stars come out. We didn't talk much. I was thinking about Mom and Dad again. I wanted to tell Marti, but I didn't know how to begin. Then I thought about our "Ann Launders" game.

There's this woman named Ann Landers, who has a newspaper column, where people write in problems and she answers them. Most of the problems reminded us of the soap operas on television, and that's why we changed the name to "Launders." Actually, that's the kind of column we hoped to write for the school paper.

So I began.

"Dear Ann Launders." One of the rules is that Ann can't say anything until the other person is finished.

"I am almost fourteen years old and live in Dullsville,

U.S.A., the armpit of the nation. There is absolutely nothing to do at night except watch Mrs. Wherle sit in her living room and drink gin and smoke pot. My formative years are losing their shape. Besides . . . my parents . . . are divorcing me. What shall I do? Emotionally Scarred."

Marti didn't gasp . . . or turn and stare at me . . . or anything. She thought for a minute, sniffed, and then answered in this voice she makes up that sounds as if she has a clothespin on her nose, "Dear Emotionally Scarred. First, get a large can of deodorant and spray all the streets. That will give you something to do and it will smell lots better in town. Second, tell Mrs. Wherle that what she is doing is reprehensible. No one can do anything about parents, so find a community project to occupy your time. Ann Launders."

Before I could say anything, Marti began again, in her own voice, "Dear Ann Launders. My problem is my parents. They *won't* get a divorce and I wish they would."

The bottom of my stomach just about fell out.

"I'm not supposed to know that they are 'holding things together for the sake of the child.' I wish to god they would let go for the sake of the child. What shall I do? Unglued."

Marti was as serious as I. She'd never said anything about her parents. I wondered what stage they were in, yelling or being polite, but I couldn't ask. That was part of the rules.

So I began in my best Mrs. Wherle voice, "Dear Unglued. That's a sticky situation. Why don't you become a juvenile delinquent and then they'll be glad to get rid of you? Ann Launders."

It wasn't very good, but it was the best I could do.

Marti laughed, though. She has this laugh that's kind of a gurgle in the back of her throat, and it always makes me laugh too.

"How about two juvenile delinquents with a community project?"

One of the things about Marti is she can almost always give me ideas that haven't been there before. So when she said that, I said, just as if I'd been planning it for weeks, "I know! The sign!"

"The sign?"

"*The* sign."

And, of course, she knew exactly what I meant, because we both thought it was so awful and so tacky. See, in the Midwest, outside of small towns, there's usually a sign with the town's name and some kind of motto. Like "Welcome Stranger to Friendly Granger" or "Peterson, the Golden Buckle on the Corn Belt" or "Sutherland, the *Little* Town with the *Big* Heart." Marti suggested they change the last word to something else that rhymed.

The sign outside of our town was worse. It said, "Dawson: Home of 3000 Good Eggs and a Few Stinkers." And it had electric light bulbs all around it that went on at sunset, automatically.

We kept hoping every Halloween that someone would rip out the light bulbs, but no one ever did. Until tonight, I'd never thought of *our* doing it.

Marti was very bright and practically never needed anything explained to her. She leaned over and whispered, "The Fuzz will be busy watching the kids in town. Let's go."

It was maybe a fifteen minute walk, and we spent the time making up nasty stories about the people we could see in the lighted windows of the houses we went past. If our stories had all been true, the town would have been closed down by the vice squad.

It was dark when we got to the edge of town and all twenty of the light bulbs edging the sign were lit. Unfortunately the sign was next to the main highway. I hadn't thought about that.

I poked Marti. "We won't have time to unscrew them. Too many cars."

"We can break them."

Good old resourceful Marti. She should have been in the CIA.

"What with?"

"Our sneakers. You get the top and right side. I'll get the bottom and other side. If we see anybody coming, we'll run for the cornfield."

It sounded easy enough, but it wasn't. We had to balance on a barbed wire fence on one foot and hold onto the sign with one hand while we swatted at the light bulbs with our sneakers. And sneakers bend a lot when you're using them for hammers.

We'd managed to knock out about half the bulbs when a car's lights showed at the top of the hill. We dived off the fence into the cornfield, which would have been okay except my T-shirt got caught on the barbed wire. Marti tried to help me unhook it, but the car kept getting closer, so I just gave a big yank and heard the shirt rip.

We must have run down the rows for half a mile before we stopped. There was a humongous hole in my shirt, which wouldn't have been so bad, except it was brand new because Mom got so tired of seeing me in my Sacajawewa shirt. We decided to tell her I'd loaned it to Marti. We did that a lot—traded clothes.

Finally, we got out of the cornfield and walked back through town, both of us a little scared that whoever was in the car had seen us.

They hadn't, for in the next evening's paper, under Police Notes were two sentences: "Unidentified vandals break 15 light bulbs on town sign. As a community project, contributions of new light bulbs will be accepted at the City Hall."

I called Marti. All she said was, "I'll bet whoever did it came unglued and is emotionally scarred."

As our "community project," we donated one fifteen-watt light bulb to the town of Dawson.

Marti said, "It's adequate reparation."

Chapter Twelve

SURE ENOUGH, MARTI AND I MADE THE FINALS OF THE town tennis tournament. I won my semi-final match, and then hung around to watch Marti play Buffi. Buffi is a dumb name, but it's better than Elvira, which is her real name and the name of her grandmother, who has lots of money.

Joan was there, and I sat beside her and we talked about my game and about how good Marti was. Joan was leaving the next day, and I hated that. It helped that Marti was home, but Joan was still somebody very special. I mean if I'd been older and there wasn't a Marti, then Joan would have been my best friend.

It didn't take Marti long to win. She did it in straight sets. Every time they changed courts, Marti bowed to the bleachers as if they were full of spectators. Sometimes Marti is an awful ham. But then Buffi's biggest interest in the game was the new tennis dress her grandmother had sent her. Marti and I wore our Sacajawewa T-shirts.

It was almost noon and the final match didn't start until four, so we had a lot of time to mess around. The only problem was what to do.

We thought of going to the pool, but in the afternoon it's full of little kids who spend all their time jumping into the water instead of swimming. The rest of the space is usually taken up by a bunch of senior girls who spread themselves out in the sun and hope the dumb lifeguards will look at them.

We sat in the grass and made a list of things we could do.

"Rob the bank?"

"They know our parents."

"Look for dirty books in the library?"

"Mrs. Wherle has them all checked out."

"Bike around the lake?"

"There isn't a lake."

"Plan our tennis game?"

"But we're playing each other."

"Sure, LC, but we have to decide who's going to win and how long it's going to take."

Marti stretched her arms out above her head. "SC, you do think of everything. Let's see. My parents will be there. They're making this big deal of doing everything together."

"Sterling."

"Reprehensible. They don't even like each other."

"Mine are coming too. Coming apart."

"For a thirteen year old, SC, that's a very good pun. Let's have you win."

I thought about that for a minute, but I knew that my winning or losing wouldn't make any real difference to anybody. Any other summer it might have, but not this summer. "No point. You win. Your folks could use it to talk about."

We figured out just how we'd do it. It wasn't like cheating or anything. Marti would never cheat. She's very responsible. It was more like writing a play. I'd win the first sets since Mom or Dad would probably have to leave before the whole match was over. Then Marti would take the next few sets until she caught up. Then after a few deuces to make it exciting, Marti would win the match. I'd be Evonne Goolagong and Marti would be Chris Evert. It's called method acting.

We split then. I went to check on Denver's water and Marti went home to change her shorts and shirt. She is a very clean person. I'm usually a little bit grubby.

I got back to the courts just as the runners-up finished their match. Joan was referee and she looked so great with her tan skin and her white shorts and shirt that when I thought about her leaving, I got the feeling of tears somewhere behind my eyes.

Marti's folks were there, sitting side by side in the top row of bleachers. They were wearing shirts that looked like they were supposed to match, but didn't quite. They looked dumb.

Marti knew exactly what I was thinking when I saw them and she nodded at me and made a face. She usually knows what I'm thinking and that makes it easy for us to be together so much. We never bore each other, and the quiet times are just as good as the exciting ones.

Mom got there just when we were volleying for service, and she sat at my end of the court. Dad came later. He sat at the other end.

Marti and I played the way we'd planned, and we winked at each other when we changed courts. Joan looked at me with a funny kind of smile, and I wondered if she knew what we were doing. After all, we'd played a lot of tennis together that summer.

One thing bothered me, though, and took my mind off what I was supposed to be doing. Mom and Dad were sitting apart from each other. Even then it seemed funny not to see them both at the same time. It was like they didn't even exist in the same world, and I got to wondering how I could be acting so normal when everything in my life was split apart. That's why I was kind of glad when they left. Not together, of course.

It was a while after that when the awful part happened. I'd quit winning and it was Marti's turn. She was really good. She was even using Chris Evert's two-handed backhand. Anyway, we were just at the point where Marti was supposed to really come through and take the match.

Maybe it would have happened if I hadn't looked up and seen Joan watching me. She wasn't smiling. She was looking surprised . . . and disappointed.

I looked back across the court at Marti, who was ready to serve. And suddenly, it wasn't Marti any more. It was just a person who was trying to beat me. I took her service and returned it cross court as low and as hard as I could. She didn't have a chance at it.

And that's the way the rest of the game went. It was as if I couldn't do anything wrong. I didn't miss any shots and I didn't make any wild ones either. I even aced some serves.

When we changed courts again, it wasn't Marti I was seeing. It was that other person whom I didn't know and I didn't care about.

I won the tournament.

It wasn't until Joan was handing me the trophy and telling me what a great game I'd played that Marti snapped back into focus. She looked at me with just a tiny bit of a smile, not at all like her usual one and said, "Congratulations."

I mumbled something about calling her after dinner and then her parents were both there, and all I wanted was to get away.

Joan caught up with me just past the root beer stand. She didn't even stop to get one . . . a root beer, I mean.

"Katie. Wait a minute."

For the first time since I'd met her, I didn't want to be with her and that made me feel even worse than before. I stopped though and waited, but I didn't look at her.

"Sit down a minute." She did and then I did too. "What's so awful about winning?"

I wanted to tell her what I had done . . . that I had betrayed Marti, but it sounded too dramatic. Just the same that's what it was—betrayal. "Marti was supposed to win. That's the way we planned it. And then it didn't happen." I couldn't tell her how Marti had turned into somebody else.

"There's no way it could have happened the way you were playing. If you'd been *honest* all the way through, she would have lost sooner."

"But she wasn't supposed to lose. Besides, she's better

than I am." And she was because she had stuck to our plan.

"Look, kid, you think you lost control, but you didn't. Maybe for the first time this summer you got some control."

Joan didn't understand and that's what I told her.

"No. You're the one who doesn't understand. Remember we've been playing tennis together twice a week, and whether you know it or not, you've been learning control. Learning, in your body, how to get in the pattern where the ball goes where you want it. Well, that's what happened this afternoon. The pattern took over. It won't always be that way, but it does happen sometimes. Once it got started, you couldn't have lost if you'd wanted to."

I nodded and felt a little bit better. It hadn't exactly been me playing. Maybe Marti hadn't been the only stranger on the court.

"But Marti . . ."

"Oh, you idiot. Marti understands. She was on the other side of the net and watched it happen. Why don't you go talk to her and find out? And come over in the morning and say good-bye to me. Okay?"

"Okay." I got up and headed toward home.

Then Joan yelled at me, "Hey, you forgot your trophy, dingy."

I went back and got it. This time I was grinning. "See you tomorrow."

But I never said good-bye to Joan because the next day I was one of the only two thirteen year olds in Dawson with hangovers.

Chapter Thirteen

WHAT HAPPENED WAS THIS. I GOT HOME AND FED AND watered Denver and went up to the house. Mom was home, and we talked about the part of the tennis game she'd watched. She didn't talk about Dad's being there. And I didn't talk about what I'd done to Marti. So we weren't really talking at all.

Then Mom broke in, "Oh, Katie. I almost forgot. Marti called while you were down with Denver. Her mother and father went into the city for dinner with some friends, and she wants to know if you'd like to stay overnight with her."

Everything was okay, at least from Marti's angle, and she wasn't mad or put out at me. Maybe I could explain to her what happened. "Is it okay with you, Mom?"

"Sure. Her parents should be home around midnight.

Have a good time and I'll see you tomorrow. Don't forget your toothbrush."

I didn't tell her that I didn't need one. That when I went over to Marti's house I shared Marti's just like she shared mine at my house. Mom would not have thought that sanitary.

But when I got to Marti's house, things didn't look right. All the curtains were pulled and I couldn't see in the front window. I opened the front door and started to walk in. I know it's not polite, but that's what we did in each other's houses. Neither of our mothers liked it very much, but they got used to it. I didn't really open the front door, though, just the front screen door. The real door was locked. No one ever locks doors in Dawson. Otherwise a neighbor couldn't get in to borrow something out of the refrigerator. For a minute I got a picture of Marti, her wrists slashed, lying on her bedroom floor all because I had betrayed her. But I should have known better. No one had ever committed suicide in Dawson. So I rang the door bell. Ours at home buzzed when anyone thought to use it. Hers went bing-bong.

It hadn't even finished the "ong" of the "bong" when Marti pulled open the door. She didn't look like any Marti I'd ever seen.

She was standing there with makeup all over her face. I mean lipstick and blusher and eyebrow pencil that had turned her blond eyebrows a muddy brown. She even had on a pair of her mother's false eyelashes, which was okay, except one of them was crooked so she looked like she was winking all the time. And she was wearing this thing that looked like a satin evening gown from a really old movie.

The dress hung over one shoulder and missed the other, and I recognized the material. It was one of the drapes that used to hang in Marti's bedroom.

She had a cigarette in one hand. It wasn't lit, but she made this really terrific motion like Joan Crawford and said, "Welcome, my dear Boobless, to a den of iniquity. And for Pete's sake come in before the neighbors see."

I scooted through the door and pushed it shut. "I didn't know it was Halloween."

She made a voice that sounded very British. "What we need, Sensitive Child, is a change of pace. Something sophisticated. Something daring. Something adult."

"I know. I've got it. You're practicing for the senior prom. But that's four years away."

"You're so naive. Go to my boudoir and become appropriately attired. You'll find things waiting for you." She motioned toward the stairs with her cigarette.

Marti's real good at acting.

"But your folks?"

"Won't be back tonight. They're staying in with some friends, and I told them I was going to your house. Soooooo. The night is young and we're so beautiful!"

That's another one of Marti's games. We'd take old songs and change the words. There's a song called "Stormy Weather." We changed it to "Sweaty sweaters. When my man and I get together. Keep sweating all the time." And there's another really old one, "Ghost Riders in the Sky." It's about a bunch of ghosts riding "up a cloudy draw." We changed it to "up a dirty bra."

I went up to Marti's bedroom and put a bunch of her mother's goop on my face. There weren't any eyelashes left, so I used mascara instead. And I used the other drape for my dress, but I looped it over the opposite shoulder. I had a little trouble keeping it up.

When I got back downstairs, Marti was still holding the cigarette, and it still wasn't lit. She had a whole pack in front of her on the coffee table. There were also two juice glasses—the plastic kind—and a bottle of something that looked like water.

"What are we doing?"

I'm more cautious than Marti.

"We are going to have an adult conversation. And this is the way adults do it. Besides we've never tried this before."

"Oh."

Marti could explain things very clearly.

We tried the cigarettes first. I lit mine, but it was the wrong end and it tasted and smelled awful. It had a filter. I took another one and that was okay as long as I didn't get any in my lungs. Marti could blow smoke out of her nose.

"How come you can do that? Did you learn at camp?"

"And leave you out? Of course not. Boobla, if you'd pay attention to the diagrams in health class, you'd know how to do it too."

"I only pay attention to the bottom half. That's more interesting."

"Depraved. That's what you are. Let's have a glass."

"A glass of what? That stuff?"

"That 'stuff' is perfectly high-class Mexican tequila that I ripped off from my folks last Christmas."

"How come you didn't tell me?"

"All in good time. And this is the *good* time."

"How do we drink it?"

"With our mouths, Boobless, with our mouths. That's explained in health class too, remember? Actually, I think we put it over ice cubes."

"They don't do that in England. At least not in movies. They always drink stuff warm."

She put out her cigarette and took another one. I'd already had two and my mouth was burning.

"You pour, Boobless."

I poured a juice glass apiece—full.

Marti raised her glass, bumped it against mine. "A toast, Madame Kathryn, to us juvenile delinquents."

We both gulped down the first swallow. I covered my mouth to keep from spitting it out and forced it down.

"Soapsuds! Lukewarm soapsuds!"

But one thing about Marti and me. We don't give up easily. Half an hour and three cigarettes later, we'd finished our glasses.

"Isn't something supposed to happen? I mean, otherwise, what's the point?"

"Maybe we didn't have enough. I'll pour this time."

"Marti? Can we open a window?"

"It wouldn't hurt. Let some of this smoke out."

The second glass tasted a little bit better than the first. At least it didn't taste worse. Then everything started moving in slow motion. The open window didn't help.

Marti tried to stand up—her first attempt at movement.

"Katie! Something's wrong. I'm sinking! Up to my ankles!"

"In . . . what?" My tongue was swollen to twice its size.

"The carpet. I think it's growing."

"Have . . . you . . . mowed it . . . lately?"

Then everything became blurry like heat waves across hot pavement. I remember insisting that Marti marry Dinty, after they'd both got out of college, and then we would be sisters. But Marti got a squinty mean look in her eyes and said that was "one-hell-of-a-sacrifice" I was demanding of her and that she didn't like Dinty any better than I did most of the time.

And that made me start to cry. Real tears. And I couldn't stop. All the tears of the summer pushed out. All the inside deadness, the anger and guilt, the screams and hate—and love—came with the tears.

"Marti," I blubbered. "I feel awful."

"Have another glass," Marti mumbled as if someone had hit her in the mouth.

Now one thing really bugs me. It's when grown people cry. That day when they signed the papers—the divorce papers—Mom went to her bedroom and cried. She didn't know I heard her. At first I was scared, and then I hated Mom for crying, and I went out to the pasture and sat under the willow the rest of the afternoon.

And now, I hated myself for crying, but I couldn't stop.

"It's all my fault, Marti."

"What is?" Marti was hunched up in her chair, her face pale.

"Every . . . thing," I sobbed. "I've done everything wrong. And now I'm being punished."

"Phooey! Punished for what?" Marti's voice sounded as if it were coming from a hollow tube.

"For all the . . . terr—ible . . . things I've done."

"You drunk or something?"

"I have done terr—ible . . . things. Like to Dinty. Like telling Mom he was with Angie Loomis . . . instead of at the Drive-In. And . . . squealing on him . . . the night he sneaked the pickup . . . one night."

"Water under the bridge, Sensitive Child." Marti yawned.

"I'm awful. Really awful," I continued blubbering. "I'm always picking on Buffi. Like giving her one hundred percent on her spelling paper when she has at least sixteen wrong, just to see Mrs. Wherle's face when Buffi gives her grade."

"Buffi never knows the difference. So . . . so who's hurt? And why . . . are you digging up all that rot?"

"Well, you're not so nice yourself. The way you answered Mrs. Wherle's questions twice. Once for her and once under your breath. Like when she asked you how was Caesar killed. And you said 'Brutus stabbed him' . . . but then you said, so she couldn't hear you, 'mixing his Caesar salad with his bayonet.' "

"That's a double intender. Gotta . . . give a right answer . . . along with a punch line . . . so they'll laugh."

"You're always jabbing Swede Kramer in the rear with your pencil, too, so Mrs. Wherle will bawl him out for wiggling."

"He keeps . . . insisting he can belch louder. When ya . . . can't beat 'em . . . you poke 'em."

"But I'm worse than you. I really am, Marti. The worst. The absolute . . . the most un . . . reprehensible."

"I don't think that's quite the correct usage, babe."

I ignored Marti and went on through my tears. "I don't

know what happened to me today. We . . . had . . . it all planned out. For you to win. And I . . . I beat you on purpose. I don't know what happened."

Marti stopped sipping and smoking and looked at me. It was a very strong and a very deep look, kind of like Mrs. Wherle when she's being her most serious. Then Marti said, making these weak, whimpering noises and clawing at her throat, then drooping over the arm of her chair, "Love means never having to say you're sorry."

I think that's when I got sick—the first time.

I stumbled back into the living room. Either it or I kept tipping slowly to one side and then to the other. Marti was still drooped over the arm of the chair.

"Dump your ashes, Lovely Child Walker, and sit up. I have a problem."

"I'm listening," she announced with a glassiness about her eyes.

So I told her how I had written the check on Mom for twenty dollars instead of twelve and how I'd spent it on tennis balls and stuff and how I'd ripped off the wristband.

Marti fingered her empty juice glass thoughtfully and then she began in her Ann Launders' voice. "Dear Guilty Conscience, So you ripped off your poor old mother. Six dollars was legit . . . for tennis supplies. You owe her two dollars. Wristband is another matter. About a dollar twenty-five. That totals three seventy-five. Why don't you give me the three seventy-five? That'll relieve your guilt complex. It is therapy, but you can call it reparation."

I fished around in my wallet, found two dollar bills and some change, and gave it to Marti without question. I never did ask Marti what she did with that money.

The last thing I remember of that terrible night was

brushing my teeth. Marti had gotten as far as the bedroom floor and collapsed. I was in the bathroom, brushing away trying to rid my mouth of the taste, and I looked in the mirror. Foam was coming out of my mouth.

I ran screaming into the bedroom. "Call an ambulance! I'm poisoned! I got rabies!"

Marti staggered to her feet, looked at me, weaving, her face inches from mine. She sniffed. Then she sneered. "Ya . . . got Dad's shaving cream . . . instead of the tooth-paste."

We lay across Marti's bed, our heads hanging over the edge.

"Boobless, ya know something?"

"I can't think. My head hurts."

"Some things ain't worth it."

"You're right," I mumbled, careful not to move.

"Most juvenile," Marti groaned and fell asleep.

Marti's parents found us the next morning—along with the evidence left in the living room. Mom arrived immediately after, her face as white as her lab coat. And Dad was standing in the front door when we got home.

"Katie," he shouted, "what the hell have you been up to?"

I could hardly hold up my head, whether from the tequila or from having to face the two of them together again, I couldn't tell.

It was hard to stay detached and attached at the same time.

I try not to remember that morning. Marti claims a person can blot out terrible things if she's willing to work at it. I do remember I got grounded until school started.

That was Mom's idea, but Dad backed her up with a "And we mean it. Until school starts."

I wanted to tell him, "*You* have no right to tell me what to do or how to live," but I didn't . . . because I knew he did.

Marti called me up later on that afternoon, after I woke up.

"Are you surviving, Sensitive Child?"

"Barely."

"Then get dressed and make yourself comfortable. We can talk via Ma Bell until they get home. You know what happened to me?"

"Don't tell me. I can't stand any more."

"I lost again. They had a private phone installed in my room. They claim I have a tendency to isolate myself from my peers. I'm not sure whether the phone is a bribe or a punishment."

"Why ask? Why couldn't I have parents that believe in bribery? I got grounded. That means quarantined until school starts."

"Man's inhumanity to man, Sensitive Child."

"What are you eating?"

"An apple. You know, Katie, even an apple tastes like tequila today."

My stomach twitched. I hung up the phone. At first I was mad. Not at Marti, but at being made a martyr, while Marti's parents gave her a private phone.

But you can keep a mad on just so long, and as the last week of that summer dragged by, I finally began to realize that if anybody was going to be responsible for me, it'd better *be me*. I wasn't responsible for Mom or for Dad or for the divorce—just for me.

One day I did a funny thing. I was cleaning out my dresser drawers—you have to do something when you're grounded—and I came across the other beaded ring I'd made in camp. I found some tissue paper, wrapped up the ring, put it in a box, wrote "To Mom" on it, and put it beside her coffee cup the next morning. I didn't understand exactly why I did it, but I felt better for doing it.

After that I quit thinking about the divorce so much. But you don't outgrow a divorce. It sticks around for a long time—maybe forever.

"So what?" Marti says. "You have an adhesive divorce. I've got adhesive parents—and I'm the glue. A child can't win."

Chapter Fourteen

I SLIPPED INTO MY SHORTS AND PULLED MY CAMP
Sacajawewa T-shirt over my head. Marti and I had
to be up at school at nine because that's when the P to Y
freshmen had to register for high school. We had decided
to wear our summer camp outfits since they were the
cruddiest things we could find. I glanced at myself in the
hall mirror—just a sideways glance—and I couldn't believe
what I saw.

I rushed downstairs to the phone. I could hardly dial
Marti's private number, my hand was shaking so.

"Marti!" I screamed into the phone. "I can't wear my
Sacajawewa shirt."

"How come? Did you dribble on it or did you wash
it with your red socks again?"

"No! *They*'re here! I finally got *them*. And *they* show."

"You mean really show? Stick out?"

"Not like Angie Loomis, but they show—on both sides."

"Sterling. Better on both sides. Otherwise you'll develop a horrible list. Very hard to walk that way. Funny I didn't notice them that night at my house."

"You spent the night on the floor, remember?"

"I was meditating."

"Mart, do you suppose it was the tequila? Or the cigarettes?"

"Probably neither. It's the shirt. It shrank."

"Listen, Marti. Can you run over with one of your bras? I can't go this way."

"Be right over. With the equipment. Anything else you need?"

"Don't be smart. And hurry up, will you?"

We were almost late for registration by the time we found enough safety pins and paper clips to get Marti's bra to stay in place. I felt like I was wearing Denver's bridle, and I had to throw my shoulders back to keep the bra from slipping. At the last minute I had to run back to get Mom's check for my fees, only I didn't run. I walked fast. Mom had left the amount blank again.

There was a long line when we finally reached the high school.

"How come you're so late?" Buffi hollered.

"Something came up," Marti answered her with a piercing look at me.

You can see Marti *is* a genius.

We finally got up to the registration desk and got this handful of junk—all sorts of forms to fill out like class schedules, student handbook with rules listed 1), 2), 3), 4).

"Too many rules, Sensitive Child," Marti announced, raising one eybrow. "Can't begin to use them all."

"How about one at a time?"

"How about one a week?" Marti studied the handbook. "For the first week let's take 'No Smoking in the Rest Rooms.' "

"They mean toilets?"

"They mean toilets, but Dawson High is never gross, my dear *Boobie*."

I let out a big laugh and felt a paper clip give and slip down the middle of my back.

"Look at me, Marti. Am I all right? Something gave."

She glanced up from the handbook. "You're holding up well. Say, *Boobie* dear, where can we get some cigarettes for the first week?"

"Dinty has some."

"Check him out. We'll need them. Now . . ." She shuffled through the forms. "First we have to fill out all this vital information like our names and ages."

"Shall we lie?"

"Of course."

So we began.

"Print, *boob*-brain. Don't write. They can't read cursive."

So I erased and started again. I got my name and address and telephone number in the proper blanks and peeked over at Marti's form.

She was on the parent–guardian part already. She was chewing the end of her pencil and gazing up at the wall. Then after "Mother's Occupation" she wrote, "Father." And after "Father's Occupation" she wrote, "Mother."

I looked down at my own form. It is very difficult to top a Marti. I thought a long time, while Marti went on to fill in her choice of subjects, with Leather Craft listed as her first choice.

I thought back on the summer . . . of the four stupid weeks at camp without Marti, of the barrel races and the city tennis tournament and of the dumb trophy, which I hid in the basement, of Joan and Grandfather and Dinty and Mom and Dad. I was glad the summer was over, and I was glad I had survived. I felt bigger—not just because of the boobs—but inside.

I took my pen and wrote after "Mother's Occupation," "Mother." And after "Father's Occupation," "Father." The last blank to complete was "Childhood Diseases." I checked every box: measles, mumps, chicken pox, whooping cough, malaria, polio, scarlet fever, and where it said, "Are you in any way physically or mentally handicapped?" I wrote in capital letters: DIVORCED.

Then I showed it to Marti.

"You're one in a million, Boobie."

"A million what?"

"One in a million kids whose parents get divorced every year. Why can't you be original? Cross it out, *Boobie*. Put in 'emotionally scarred.' You could get excused from Phys. Ed for that."

So I did.

We sorted out our completed forms and walked over to the main office. Marti pushed open the door, and there, grinning at us, her hands planted on the desk was—Mrs. Wherle—with a "Hello, girls."

We escaped, walking as fast as my inner harness

would allow, and then running full speed down the two flights of stone steps that led from Dawson High School.

"My god. Somebody promoted Wherle, too!" Marti had both hands in her hair as if she were doing a Bette Davis mad act.

"*Boobie,*" she cried, putting her arm around my neck in a wrestling hold and ripping loose the last safety pin from my bra. "It's going to be a long four years."

Martha (Marti) Walker.

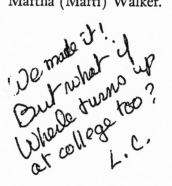

'We made it!.. But what if Where turns up at college too? L.C.

"Sterling, but reprehensible." Newspaper: 1, 2, 3, 4. Editor, 4. Assistant Editor *Bomb*, 4. Tennis Team: 1, 2, 3, 4. Honor Society: 3, 4. Student Council President, 4. Thespians: 1, 2, 3, 4. Outstanding Actress Award, 4. Future Plans: Life.

THE DAWSON HIGH SCHOOL BOMB

Senior Page

Kathryn (Boobie) Warner.

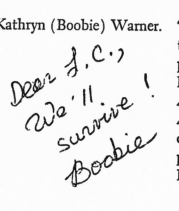

Dear J.C., We'll survive! Boobie

"I'd rather be a stinker than a good egg." Newspaper: 1, 2, 3, 4. Assistant Editor, 4. *Bomb* Editor 4. Tennis Team: 1, 2, 3, 4. Honor Society: 4. Student Council: 4. Thespians: 1, 2, 3, 4. Future Plans: Brain Surgeon.